LIMINAL SPACE

LIMINAL SPACE
FICTION FROM THE SLIPSTREAM

by

Jackie Gamber

For Stephen Bailey
Your encouragement opens the curtain
to let in the light

CONTENTS

LIMINAL SPACE

HIDDEN
THE LOST WORKS OF DERNELL HALL

Dernell Hall was born with his eyes open. He came out headfirst like most babies do, splashed into the warm water of the hospital's birthing pool, and sucked in his first breath just as he was laid on Mama's chest, all the while staring up at hovering faces with brown and bloodshot eyes.

"Look at him thinking," said Dernell's daddy, stroking his son's wet spine.

"He's so pale, he looks like a white baby," said Aunt Jojo, his mama's sister, who'd been there watching.

"He'll darken soon enough," said Mama, and lifted her chin to kiss her husband's mouth. "He'll get his cinnamon color from his daddy."

"But not his name?" asked Aunt Jojo.

"This boy is Dernell," said Daddy. And that was that.

§

Dernell scooted his chubby bottom down the carpet steps, listening to the shwoop of his diaper. He was suddenly startled by pain. He'd grazed his thigh over a loose nail in the banister, and a trickle of bright color rose up through a crack in his smooth skin. He touched the color. It transferred to his finger. He pressed his finger against the white wall. It made a mark that looked so much like the bump on Daddy's nose that Dernell couldn't help but pat, pat, pat that bright color in a hazy pattern that mimicked the furrows and valleys of Daddy's whole face. He was just poking a finishing touch at the corner of Daddy's eye when Mama came.

"Oh, Dernell! Oh, baby! What have you done to yourself?" She scooped him off the step and turned him over to look at his bleeding scratch.

Dernell gurgled and pointed to Daddy's face on the wall.

Mama just grabbed the phone and babbled hysterically at Aunt Jojo.

§

Dernell sidled up to two girls drawing white chalk squares on the sidewalk during recess.

When the girls tossed the chalk into the grass and began hopping back and forth across the squares, Dernell watched the chalk, and the way the morning dew speckled the glossy sides of the white stick.

Then he pressed the end of the stick to the pavement, and swirled great, wavy lines. Using the dark spots on the chalk to make shadows, and the light parts of the chalk to make highlights, Dernell rendered the snowy peaks of the mountains majesty that came to his mind's eye whenever he sang his favorite song in school.

The recess bell rang.

"Mrs. Donovan," wailed one of the hopscotch girls. "Dernell stole our chalk!"

Mrs. Donovan bore down on Dernell like a stalking cougar from his drawn mountains. "Young man, what do you have to say for yourself?"

Dernell pointed to his sidewalk art, but no one was looking at it.

They were puffy-faced and staring only at him.

He skulked inside.

§

"I like to draw," Dernell confessed at the dinner table.

His parents and his little sister all regarded him.

"As long as you keep up with homework," said Daddy.

"I wondered where all our pencils kept going," said Mama.

"I like Math," said his sister. She poked at her mashed potatoes with her spoon.

"I put in a picture for the art show at school," said

Dernell. "I worked two weeks straight on it."

"What's the picture?" asked Mama.

"Therese," he said, pointing to his little sister, who grinned at him. "From last summer when she was blowing bubbles off the front porch. Her lips are all puckered, and her eyes are closed because she's afraid a bubble will pop and sting her eyes."

His sister giggled. "I remember that."

"When's this art show?" asked Daddy.

"Saturday in the gym. Will you go see it?"

"Of course," said Mama. "I'll be real proud."

On Saturday Dernell could hardly breathe, he was so nervous. He was the first of the family into the gym, his hands clenched to fists so he wouldn't fidget. He found his picture immediately and sucked in a breath to see it right where he'd put it, hung between Dory McCallister's pastel daylilies and Ethan Smith's oil painting of a sunset. Dernell's art was all pencil, so it contrasted the others, but he chose it that way. He stared, frozen in fear and anticipation, as his family came up behind him.

"Look at all these pictures," said Mama. "I never knew you had so much talent in your school, Dernell."

"I like the flowers," said Therese, and pointed to Dory's drawing. "Can you draw me some flowers for my room, Dernell?"

"There are copper sculptures over there," said Daddy. "I wonder if they sell this stuff."

Off his parents shuffled, with Therese bouncing between them.

"But..." said Dernell, his voice fading behind them.

§

At the school bus stop, a cardinal fluttered to a wobbly landing on a nearby willow branch. It cocked its crimson head and stared right into Dernell's eyes.

Dernell's hand dipped into his backpack for a notepad and pencil. He met the cardinal's gaze and sketched.

"What are you writing?" asked Brittney Cole, her voice coming from around his shoulder, her soft hair tickling his arm while she peeked.

"Drawing," Dernell said, distracted by the challenging angle of the cardinal's beak.

"You're an artist?"

His hand paused. He looked at the top of her head, and at the way the sunlight glistened her painted highlights. "I draw, anyway."

She tipped up her face, and her wrinkled brows. She looked back at his paper, and again to his face. "Draw what?" she asked.

The bus pulled up with a hiss of air brakes, and the cardinal flustered away.

"The bird," said Dernell, pointing to his sketch, but Brittney was already climbing with silky legs, pale like sidewalk chalk, into the school bus. He looked again at his drawing, ran his fingers over it.

Graphite smudged their tips, and he studied it.

He put his fingers to his tongue and tasted it. It

was there. He was sure of it.

§

On Saturday, Dernell had harnessed himself into a hardware store rope and was dangling against the side of the old penny candy store.

The building was more rubble than brick but situated at the curve of a road that no passerby failed to notice.

Dernell had two of Mama's pocketed aprons lashed front and back around his waist. They were stuffed with spray paint. He swung back and forth, squirting color and shadow against the crumbling brick, determined to create a masterpiece the whole town could see.

The morning sun blazed high and hot, drying the paint almost the instant it touched the wall. He swooped red for a cardinal perched on a soap bubble. He gave short bursts of silver for the shine of those bubbles blown by Therese's puckered mouth. He pushed off with his feet to sway over the background of purple mountains bursting through clouds, and layered more cinnamon brown for the skin of Daddy's laughing face. Perspiration was making it hard to grip the cans, but he worked long into the afternoon anyway.

Then a siren yowled briefly from below and snapped off. "Son," said a voice through a speaker. "This is Officer Stanton. Your parents are on their way."

Dernell drew his forearm across his brow and gazed down at the blob of uniform beside a black and white police car. "Okay," he called. "I was just finishing."

"They told me they love you very much and want you to hang on until they get here," said Officer Stanton into his radio mouthpiece. "Whatever it is, we can talk you through it."

A grumble of engine brought his parents' Sonata into view. They pulled up beside the police car, and Mama climbed out first. "Dernell!"

"Hold on, son," hollered Daddy. "Just hold on!"

"Hi," said Dernell, and pointed over his shoulder to his 20-foot mural. "Do you like it?"

"What's he saying?" asked Mama, clutching at Daddy's arm.

Dernell had thought he might get into trouble for defacing public property or something, but he hadn't expected the worried looks on his parents' faces. "What's the matter, isn't it good?" he called.

"Yes," called Officer Stanton. "You're good, son. Of course you are."

Mama grabbed the radio piece from the officer and squealed into it, "Dernell, don't let go! You know we love you baby. Whatever's troubling you, we'll get through it together!"

"What?" asked Dernell.

More sirens screeched, muffled by distance and treetops, but they were getting closer. Soon an ambulance and a fire truck shambled around the crowded corner and jerked to a stop. Firemen spilled out from the truck like cockroaches, shouting to each other and bustling with equipment.

"I just wanted you to see my art," shouted Dernell.

"We'll get you the help you need," said Mama, tears in her voice. "I know it's been hard as a Black boy in a White community."

Daddy stole the mouthpiece and frothed into it. "I spent too many hours at the office. I failed you."

Dernell pulled a paint can from Mama's apron and waved it around. "I just wanted you to see my art!"

A ladder burst out from the top of the fire truck. A man, decked in helmet and goggles, waved his arms from inside a large basket at the end. "Don't be afraid," he said. "Let me help you."

"Isn't anyone going to say anything about my mural?" Dernell called.

The ladder stopped. The fireman pursed his lips, squeezing his blonde mustache into a furry wrinkle. He eyed the wall, then looked back at Dernell. "Mural?"

Dernell held up his paint can. "I painted it with this." His sweaty finger slipped, and he squirted a brown fan onto the man's goggles, right across his line of vision. Dernell gasped.

The man blinked. Then he smiled. "Eh, right. Okay, son. You did a good job painting, now it's time to go home." He pulled Dernell into the ladder basket and hacked at the rope. Then he gestured to someone Dernell couldn't see, and the ladder shriveled downward.

"Oh baby!" cried Mama when Dernell touched earth, running toward him to hug him.

Daddy squeezed him too, smothering Dernell's face in the crook of his arm.

"I'm okay," he muttered.

"Thank God you didn't jump," said Mama. "Thank God you didn't jump."

"What?"

"Mr. and Mrs. Hall?" said Officer Stanton. They released Dernell and turned. "Standard procedure is to get him to a hospital now. You can take him in your own car, if you like."

"Thank you, officer," said Daddy.

"Why do I need to go to a hospital?" asked Dernell. "I'm not hurt."

"No, you're not," said Officer Stanton. "Thanks to Buddy, here." He pulled over the fireman who'd helped Dernell onto the ladder. The fireman with brown paint across his goggles.

"Just doing my job," said Buddy.

The three shuffled toward their car, Mama crying and Daddy telling her everything was going to be okay. Dernell's head was spinning. Then he heard Buddy, and he looked over his shoulder to see the fireman leaning toward Officer Stanton to whisper.

"Hey, someone should tell the doc at the hospital there's more going on here than a suicide attempt. Kid's hallucinating or something. He was up there trying to deface the building with empty cans of spray paint."

Officer Stanton turned narrowed eyes to Dernell. Dernell looked away. The car door closed between them.

Dernell laid his head back against the seat. "I just wanted someone to see my art," he said.

Mama patted Daddy's shoulder, her fingers

trembling. "Dernell likes to draw."

LINCOLN'S CALL

The scent of Lincoln Asfeld's grief emanated from his pores, bled through each fiber of his clothes. It lingered in the air even after he'd passed.

Strangers in the street who unknowingly stepped into his wake took on a gloominess, lifted their nose to the wind, and commented on expected rain.

It had been four unremarkable years since Janet had died. To the date, in fact, for she'd had the ironic timing to die on her own birthday, and today was Janet's birthday.

Lincoln knew this, not because he'd looked at a calendar. Not because it was brighter or gloomier or any different from every other day this year. He knew because of the birthday card addressed to Janet that trembled in his fingertips like a final, parched maple leaf in the autumn wind.

He leaned against his fridge, staring once more at the intricate design on the card's front page.

Perky bluebirds swept a yellow ribbon above the words.

Janet had loved bluebirds. Her collection still reigned on the second shelf of his bedroom bookcase, meticulously dusted.

He stuck the card to the freezer with a fat magnet. Then he tugged open the door to find the bottle of Ketel One vodka he kept beside the stack of frozen dinners and cookie dough ice cream. He didn't bother with a glass. Just one more thing to wash. He lowered himself into a chair with all the heaviness of a man twice his weight.

For three years now he'd faced the day of his wife's birth and death with a cheerful card from his sister. And he would call his sister to explain once more to her feeble mind that Janet was dead.

Brain cancer. From the first headache to the last breath had been a brief and painful three weeks.

He'd remind his sister she'd been to the funeral, threw handfuls of damp dirt over the casket, greeted well-wishers at the wake, and sat with him and wept.

And she would remember, and weep anew. And apologize.

The vodka bottle warmed against his hand and sent beads of moisture across his knuckles. His eyes lingered on the bluebirds on the fridge. Then the bottle raised, pressed to his pale lips, and was emptied.

He reached for the phone.

PAST PERFECT

"I don't do that kind of thing anymore, Roger. You of all people should know that." I leaned back in the booth and waved to catch the attention of the waitress for a refill of my Bud Light.

"I know I shouldn't be asking. But this girl is going out of her mind. The police have chalked it up to a random burglary gone bad, and she keeps calling to find out if they've got any more leads, but they put her on hold or pass her around." Roger laid down his fork. "Her only sister. And the guy who killed her is going to get away with it." He glanced up at the waitress, who appeared at the table with a pitcher and leaned over to refill my glass. He raked his fingers through his thinning hair. When she disappeared again, he leaned forward. "Mick. Come on, man. He's going to get away with it."

For a split second, a familiar pang sparked in my

stomach. I guzzled my beer to extinguish it.

"All I'm asking you to do is talk with her." Roger wrapped thick fingers around his own glass. "Maybe you can't even help, I'm just asking you to find out."

"I can't help her, Rog," I started to say, when a sudden "Oh my gosh" squealed from across the room. We both turned. Our waitress was bouncing toward the table with a book in her hands.

"Duck and cover," Rog mumbled.

"I can't believe it," said the waitress, breathless, as she reached our table. A blonde strand had pulled from her braid to dangle into her eyes, and she brushed it away. "I've been serving you all night. I can't believe I didn't recognize you. My manager did, though."

I glanced at Roger, who quietly sipped and laughed at me with his eyes.

"I want to be a writer, too," the waitress said. "I'm just working here to get through school." She smiled. She absently turned the book in her hands. "I've read all your books, and I'm halfway through this one. I'm taking my time because it's the last one."

Now I just wanted to be home, drinking alone in front of the tv. "Look," I said. "Did you want me to…?" I reached for her book.

She squealed again, and pressed it into my hands. "Oh my gosh, would you? I'm Staci. With an "i". Can I sit down?"

I fumbled in my pocket for a pen. Staci produced one from somewhere down her shirt.

"You bet you can, Staci-with-an-i," said Roger, just

as I was signing my name on the title page. I glared. He ignored me. "Unless your boyfriend would get jealous. A pretty girl like you must have a boyfriend."

Staci slid into the booth beside me with a giggle. "Oh, he won't mind. He's nobody serious, anyway." Her hand rested on my thigh.

I shifted, and pushed the book back at her. "Could we get our check, please?"

"So, Staci," said Rog. "Who got you turned on to Mick's books?"

"A girlfriend of mine. I never read any true crime stuff before, but she said he writes more like a novelist, really, and she was right." Staci lowered her chin, and gazed up at me. "I start reading, and I can't put it down. It's like I'm right there in the room, watching each murder happen. I know the victim like I know my own friend, and then I have to watch her die." She sighed, and rested her hand on the book cover. "I grieve, you know?"

"Yeah," I said.

"The way you write, Mr. Berkley, it's a gift. I swear, it's…it's like, this spiritual thing, or something." Her hand found my thigh again. I shifted again.

"Call him Mick," said Roger.

"Mick," she said, smiling at me. "I wish you'd write another one."

"No, I'm through with that."

"Maybe you've lost your inspiration. Maybe you need a muse." Her fingers brushed the top of my knee.

"What I really need right now is the check," I said.

She looked at Roger, then back at me. She slid out of the booth. "I'll be right back with that." Then she breathed my name. "Mick." She smiled, and casually moved toward the kitchen. In the archway, girls' faces peered out, watching. As she neared them, she lifted the signed book and waved it in triumph. Giggles broke out, and they all clamored to see it.

"You are something else," said Roger. "You're scaring me, man."

"What are you talking about?"

"I'm talking about Staci-with-an-i. She's practically in your lap, and you ask for the check. You're a freaking zombie."

I looked where the waitress disappeared into the kitchen. "She's a kid, Rog. She's half my age."

Roger laughed. "You're not that old yet. You just act like it." He drained his glass. "She was feeling you up under the table, wasn't she?"

"Could we just drop it?"

Just then, Staci was there. She slid the bill across the table. "I didn't charge you for the refills." She winked, and then slipped away.

When Roger looked over the bill, his face curled into a wide grin. "She's right, she didn't charge us. By the way, she gets off at nine. Want her phone number?" He held up the slip of paper for me to see her handwritten note.

"You keep it," I said.

Roger shook his head. "I'm already meeting someone tonight." He dug his wallet out of his back pocket, and held it for a minute. "What do I tell her when I see her? Are you going to help?"

"You know I can't."

"Come on, Mick. Have I ever asked you for anything, in all the years you've known me?"

"You borrowed my golf clubs last week. I haven't gotten them back yet, by the way."

"What do you need them for? You haven't golfed in years. You haven't bought a new shirt, haven't seen a movie. You used to hike, remember that? Now I have to bribe you out of the house by buying you dinner."

"If you buying means I have to listen to a lecture, I'll gladly pay for my own steak." I tried to snatch the bill, but Roger dodged.

"You've been living in a studio while you pay the mortgage on a house no one lives in, man. The house. Your stuff is still there. Her stuff is still there. That doesn't tell you something?"

Now the pang was back, smoldering in my ribs, and I didn't have a beer. "You're saying this to me? You, Rog?" I slid out of the booth, and dug cash out of my shirt pocket. "Don't buy me any more steaks. Don't do me any more favors."

Roger held up his hands. "Hey, don't do that. I said I'd pay, I'll pay. Mick, come on." He pushed my twenty back toward my pocket. "You know I'm just worried about you. It's been four years, and you're still dead to the world. When are you going to let it go? When are you going to live?"

I tossed my twenty onto the table. "I don't do that

kind of thing anymore."

I woke with a headache. It wasn't beer; I'd only had two last night. It was just the way I woke up. Always like I hadn't slept at all. Always with a headache. I reached for the bottle of Excedrin on the floor.

I was chewing four of them when my speaker buzzed. The foot of my bed was six feet from the only door, but I didn't feel like walking the distance. Besides, it was only Roger checking in, and I didn't want to talk to him. Last night was a low blow. My best friend, chewing on me like everyone else about how to live.

The speaker buzzed again, and again, and then held the droning note until it bored into the base of skull. I threw myself out of bed and hammered my fist on the button. "Go away, Rog!"

The buzzer sounded again, but I ignored it. Maybe if Roger stood out there in the cold morning, his fingers would get too numb to buzz anymore. I had more important things to do right now, like find coffee. I looked in the cupboard where coffee ought to be, but found only a can with a few hopeless-looking grounds in the bottom.

A knock sounded on the door. "Mr. Berkley?"

What the…? I stared at the door, frozen.

"Michael Berkley? I'm Annette Caldwell. I'm a friend of Roger Stein."

What was Roger doing, giving my address to strangers? Had he lost his mind?

"He said you like Starbucks French roast. I've got

some here. And a bagel."

Oh, that was downright cunning. I inched toward the door. "Cream cheese?"

"Onion and chive."

I grumbled. I unlatched the door and swung it open to face the woman. I glared, one hand on my hip, brandishing my morning hair and faded boxers. She didn't flinch.

"Someone let me in downstairs. I'm really sorry to disturb you at home." She offered a cardboard carrier, and I reluctantly plucked out my coffee bribe.

"Roger shouldn't have told you where I live."

"He didn't." As she strode in, her eyes swept the place. The trashcan was so full the lid wouldn't close. Sticky dishes piled high in the tiny sink. Power bar wrappers littered the carpet, and I couldn't remember the last time I vacuumed. Funny how you don't notice things until someone else does.

She took her own coffee, and set the empty carrier and a brown paper bag on the counter. She carried her drink toward a chair, swept a couple of socks and a shirt off the cushion, and sat down. "I was at the restaurant last night. I followed you here."

Peeling back the lid from my cup, I paused. "You what?"

"Roger didn't know."

"He was supposed to tell you I can't help you."

"He did." She gently blew across her coffee, and crossed her legs. She was wearing a blue plaid skirt and knee-high leather boots. Her blue sweater turned her eyes a vivid sapphire, and I moved closer to get a better look. How long had it been since I'd noticed a woman's eyes?

"Then why are you here?" I asked.

"I don't take no for an answer," she said.

"If you were a man, I'd call you cocky."

"I'm a lawyer."

"Oh. That explains it."

She nodded and took a sip of coffee. "I've been hounding the police for weeks now. Every lead they've followed has been a dead-end. They say my sister came home to a burglar and he killed her, but left everything she owned behind. Even our mom's emerald ring she kept in her nightstand."

"Maybe he knew not to bother hocking anything, for fear of being traced."

"Maybe. Except, a couple weeks before she died, my sister told me someone was following her. A man kept showing up wherever she went, and…"

I drew a bagel, the cream cheese, and a plastic knife out of the bag. I popped the lid and smeared onion and chive over the soft bread. "And what?"

"I don't know. I think he was in her apartment once before. She was getting really freaked out, and I'd told her she needed to talk to the police, but she didn't. The whole thing is just so unbelievable." She lowered her coffee, and then her chin. She touched her fingers to her closed eyelids.

I chewed for a while, watching her. I would have sympathized with her if I could, and a part of me wanted to. But then I would have to feel again, and I couldn't bring myself to do it.

I walked to my bed and hoisted it, messy sheets and all, into the spring-loaded cubby in the wall that held it. I closed the closet doors around it, then pushed the couch back into the middle of the room to sit.

"Roger told me about your wife," she said quietly. "He said you never went back to being a private eye, and you never wrote another word after she was murdered."

"You're right. I don't investigate anymore, which is why I can't help you."

"He said you told the police who did it. You saw him do it. But they've never been able to prove it."

I stood. "You'd better go."

She didn't move. "The police say you weren't there that night, so you couldn't have seen him."

"I won't talk about this with you." My hands began to shake around my coffee cup.

"How did you see him, Mr. Berkley? If you weren't there, how could you describe his face so vividly to the cops?"

My lungs tightened like I'd just climbed three flights of stairs. "I'm warning you. If you don't leave right now, I'll pick you up, chair and all, and throw you out."

She did stand, but she only moved closer, and stared at me with eyes of blue steel. "I'm reading your books. Every one has details you couldn't possibly know, no matter how brilliant an investigator you are. You even led police to clues they hadn't found. Every book reads as though I'm standing in the room, watching it happen. As though you're in the room, Mr. Berkley. As though you're watching it happen."

My heart pounded so hard against my chest that it hurt. I clenched my fists. Hot French roast splattered against my boxers and ran down my knee. My hand shook, still holding the crushed insulated cup. "Get out," I growled.

She reached for the door. "I think club soda will get that coffee out of your carpet." She closed the door behind herself.

I don't know how long I stared at the door, trying to get ahold of myself. I'd come so close to grabbing her by her hair and throwing her out into the hall that I'd startled myself. I tried to breathe, tried to slow my heartbeat, tried to remember if I had any beer in the fridge.

Then I noticed she'd left her coffee behind. Fine. She owed it to me, anyway. I just hoped she hadn't watered it down with cream or sugar. Lifting it from the chair, I saw she'd also left her purse. It was a small bag, woven like macramé, with dangling ivory beads. I groaned. The coffee she wouldn't return for, but the purse she might. Better to try to catch her before she left the building. I didn't want her to have any reason to come back.

I grabbed the bag and ran for the door, but suddenly stopped, feeling a dizzy sensation that I hadn't felt in years. I clutched at the doorknob, but it disappeared in my hand. All around me, the walls melted and dribbled like wax to the floor. Then the floor evaporated, and I was standing at the curb of a busy downtown street.

People bustle all around me. A man stops to check his watch, then folds a newspaper under his arm. He adjusts his tie as he passes.

A woman leans out from a storefront. She's waving to someone I can't see.

I smell hot dogs and mustard and turn to find a corner vendor open a cart lid and laugh. Steam billows out and obscures his face. Horns honk. A bike bell chimes.

"Taxi!" calls a voice beside me.

Somehow, I know her voice, and I don't want to look, but I must.

She's standing so closely I can smell her Giorgio knock-off perfume, and when her dark hair flutters in a gust of cold wind, I feel it tickle my cheek. She faces me and calls again for a taxi.

I catch my breath. She has her sister's chin and cheekbones, but her eyes are dark, and softer. She's wearing no eye shadow, no liner, no makeup at all on her glowing face, except a shine of raspberry gloss. A strand of her hair blows across the gloss, and sticks there. She tugs it away.

Then she frowns. Her shoulders stiffen. She peers behind herself as though she senses someone watching. She looks to her left, to her right. She looks toward me, but through me, because I'm not seen.

I'm the Ghost of Christmas Past. I watch, but cannot be watched. I'm surrounded by the smells and sounds and tastes of life, but it isn't real. This woman I observe as she nibbles her bottom lip is dead. I remind myself that she's dead.

She falters at the edge of the curb, and I dart out a hand to steady her anyway. My hand passes right through. She finds her balance, and laughs a little, glancing around to see who noticed. Her eyes catch on a shadowed man near an alley. Her frown returns.

A taxi shrieks to a halt beside her.

"Thank you," she says, and digs around in a small purse over her arm. The bag is woven like macramé, and dangles with ivory beads. "I need to get to Broadway and 6th."

"So get in," snaps the driver.

"Wait!" comes a woman's ragged voice in the distance. "Oh, wait! Please! I need that taxi!"

This woman steps back, and shields her eyes with her hand. "I'm late for something, but we can share."

"Oh, bless you. Bless you." An elderly woman staggers into view and grasps the woman's hand. "Bless you," she says again.

The vision crumbled, and I stood again at the door of my apartment. I dropped to my knees, nauseated, tasting bile in my throat. I used to be accustomed to the sickening feeling of shifting, like a drop on a roller coaster, but I hadn't done it in so long, I wasn't used to it anymore.

I clutched the macramé bag in my hand. I turned it over, staring at it. Coincidence? Did Annette use her sister's purse for her own, and leave it behind in her hurry to leave? Somehow, I didn't think so. I opened it. Inside, lying against the satin lining was only one item. A business card.

Annette Caldwell's business card. I flipped it over. It read, "I know you saw her. Call me."

I threw the purse across the room.

§

My cell phone blasted its rendition of Beethoven's Fifth.

I let it get to the reprise before I flopped off the couch and crawled to where the phone was clipped to my jeans, left in a pile where I slid them off last night. I checked the caller ID. Rog. I almost didn't answer.

"Yeah?" I said into the phone.

"Mick, are you sleeping? What's the deal? It's three o'clock."

I yawned. "So?"

"So, it's Thursday. Three o'clock. I'm at the gym, and you're not."

"Oh, crap." I looked at my wrist, but I wasn't wearing a watch. "Man, I forgot."

I heard muffled voices through his hand over the mouthpiece, and then he was back. "Ok, I've got to get back to work, anyway, so don't bother coming now. I'll reschedule again, but if you're a no-show the third time, we'll just forget it. We're supposed to be doing this together."

"I know, Rog. I'm sorry."

He was silent for a minute. "Hey, uh… did Annette talk to you about her sister?"

"Yeah. Armed with Starbucks, no less."

"I didn't put her up to that, you know," he said.

"I know. She's got major cojones. I see why you like her."

Roger laughed. "Yeah, well. She goes after what she wants."

"Hey… did you tell her about me? About what happens when I touch dead people's stuff?"

"No way. You know I wouldn't. It'd make me sound crazier than you."

"Yeah. Okay. I'll talk to you later."

I closed the phone. I sat wondering how Annette Caldwell knew to leave her sister's purse for me. I believed Roger. In all the years I'd known him, he'd never told anyone about my shifts. But Annette knew somehow.

Or did she? Maybe in her mind, she'd put some puzzle pieces together, and took a wild, desperate guess. That would be easy to play off. If I hadn't had a vision, I wouldn't have understood the note, and would have no reason to call her back. Her gamble didn't work, and I was off the hook.

Except that I had a purse she'd left behind. Any decent person would find the business card inside and give her a call, just to let her know. I considered myself a decent person. So by not calling, it was the same as admitting I was hiding something. She'd know I found the note and understood it, and that's why I wasn't calling back.

Either way, she had me.

I stewed. I brooded. Finally, I sighed. I crawled to the purse on the floor, dug out the business card again, and flipped open my phone. I would be nonchalant. Just act like I'd found this bag of hers, and did she want it back? No big deal, I'd just pass it on to Rog. Sure, you're welcome.

"Hello, this is Annette."

"Hey, Annette. This is Mick Berkley. The other day when you were over—"

"I knew you'd call." Her voice was soft.

"Yeah? Well, I think you left a purse—"

"You know I did. And you know it's not mine."

I shifted the phone against my ear. I cleared my throat to try again. "Anyway, I just thought if you want it back, I could give it to Rog next time I—"

"Are you at home?"

I blinked. "What?"

"I'm actually just around the corner from your apartment. I'll be there in five."

She hung up.

I stared at the phone, trying to figure out what just happened. Then I bolted up and grabbed my jeans. I splashed some water on my face, ran my wet hands through my hair, and tugged a shirt over my head as I closed the apartment door behind me.

There was a seat in Buford's Sandwich Shop across the street that had an excellent view of my apartment steps. I'd used it plenty of times to watch for reporters, or fans, or, more often lately, creditors. This time, I would watch Annette Caldwell try to get inside, find me gone, and then give up. I'd poke at a tuna salad until the coast was clear, and then go back home and finish my afternoon nap.

I made it outside, and realized I'd forgotten my jacket. Cool air crept right through my cotton shirt, and I tucked my hands under my armpits.

"Michael!" I heard her call, but pretended I didn't. I darted toward the street.

I dodged cars, jumped to avoid a kid on a skateboard, and finally made it to the door of my sandwich shop. Annette was there, glaring at me, her arms crossed. "You look cold."

"I am."

She held up my book. "If you don't give me ten minutes of your time, I'm going to announce a book signing with author Michael Berkley beginning immediately."

I shrank back. "You wouldn't."

She waved the book. "Attention everyone!"

I clutched her elbow and pushed her into Buford's. "You're cold. Downright cold."

"You're the one with blue lips," she said.

We found a small table in the back. I ordered my tuna salad and water, and she ordered a Reuben and iced tea. I'd make sure she paid the bill, for all the trouble she was causing.

"So what did you want to talk to me about?" I asked, trying to open the wrapper around my spork.

She opened a packet of sugar into her iced tea. "What did you see when you touched my sister's purse?"

I thought I was prepared for the question, but I stabbed myself on plastic tines, anyway. "I don't know what you're talking about."

She narrowed her eyes. Then she pulled out a small locket. "I got this for her 26th birthday present. She was wearing it when she was killed a week later. Look inside it."

"Why? What's in it?"

"Find out."

I regarded the locket. I turned my eyes to Annette. Then I shook my head. "You're baiting me."

"Baiting you? By asking you to touch Sarah's locket? Why should that be a problem?"

Our sandwiches arrived.

I was glad for the distraction, and was considering asking to have mine wrapped to go.

But Annette put the locket back into her pocket, and silently sliced her Reuben in half.

"That was her name?" I asked. "Sarah?"

She nodded.

"I'd been wondering."

"I always thought it suited her. It's such a pretty name, in an innocent kind of way. She always trusted people, and never played the mind games the rest of us are so good at." She set her plastic knife down. "I was sort of jealous of her for that. I get the things I want by playing the game, you know? But she didn't."

I peeled off the top bread from my sandwich and ate a sporkful of tuna.

"She was an artist. She loved spicy chili. We couldn't have been more different if we tried, but we were close, anyway. You know, she hardly ever wore makeup, except a little lip-gloss, but men noticed her. She didn't know they did, half the time. She was so beautiful. Don't you think?"

Like her sister, but softer. Like my Dee, but younger. "Yeah," I said.

She crossed her arms and leaned back in her chair.

I realized what I'd just done. "I mean, she sounds—"

She waved her hand. "Oh, please. Don't." She leaned forward. "You have a gift. It's a part of you, Michael, and it won't go away by denying it."

"Don't call me Michael."

"Fine. Mick. Mickey. Mickey Mouse, more like it."

"Don't think you know anything about me," I said, stabbing at my sandwich. "Call it a gift, if you want, whatever that is you think you've figured out about me, but it's no gift."

"It could be. You could be using it to help people, like you did before."

"Don't you get it?" I spit a hot whisper into her face. "Who did I help? Angela, who they found tied to her ceiling fan? Francine, who they found in the boiler room of her apartment building? All I could do was stare and watch it happen, and I couldn't do one thing to stop it. I couldn't even save Dee. I couldn't even help my own wife."

I stood up so fast, I knocked over her tea glass.

She yelped, and a waitress scuttled over to help, but I stomped toward the door.

I didn't care. Let her drown in it.

I surged toward the street. Dee's face kept trying to find its way behind my eyes, and I forced it back. I couldn't look at it anymore. I couldn't stand to see her mouth, wide open in a scream, and her pale eyes gone wild with terror.

A horn blared, but I barely heard it. Brakes squealed. Hands grabbed my arms and yanked me hard.

I looked up to see a cabdriver lean out his window and holler at me. The front of his car had come to stop at the place where I'd just been standing.

"Mick, come on, get out of the street." Annette tugged me again, toward the sidewalk. "I'm sorry. I wasn't even thinking about you in all this, I was only thinking about myself, and my own pain. I'm so sorry."

I heard her, but all I could see was Dee. "I can't. Don't ask me to look again. I can't stand to watch anymore."

Her arms wrapped my neck, and I was swallowed by her softness. Her cheek pressed to mine. Her cashmere jacket hugged me front to back, and I shivered. "You're still cold," she said.

I nodded, and drew my hands down her sides to bury my chilly fingers into her pockets.

Dee's face began to fade.

I could almost breathe again. My left hand touched something round in Annette's pocket. I ran my thumb over it, trying to figure it out. Then the busy scene around me trickled away, and the city sidewalk became smooth tile beneath my feet.

I'm standing outside a toy store in the mall. A stuffed, mechanical dog yips incessantly, and tries to walk off the end of a display table. A plastic army man crawls on his belly but can't go anywhere because he's tied to the table leg. His tiny machine gun rattles gunfire at passing civilians.

I smell the spice of warm gyros and hear the hot crackle of submerged corn dogs. Someone carries a plastic tray with fries and a bubbling drink to a bench. People surround me, crowd around me, bustle right through me.

I hear her laugh, and turn to find her, but she's nowhere in the swarm of faces that pass. I try to follow the sound. She laughs again. It's a rich and throaty sound, unabashed. I spot pink tennis shoes under the curtain of a picture booth, and close in.

The pink shoes scuffle. The curtain moves aside. I see her then, in white shorts and a pink blouse. A brassy locket dangles from her hand. Her dark hair is swept into a ponytail that turns on itself and is tucked again through a pink elastic band.

I creep closer. She bends to poke her finger at the slot where her developed photos will emerge, and my eyes follow the curve of her hamstring. Her skin looks so smooth, it's like Barbie doll vinyl.

"You have to give it a minute." Annette's voice comes from the photo booth, and then her blonde head pokes out and she smiles.

"They can send a robot to Mars, but they can't get instant pictures from a photo booth?" Sarah turns her back and leans against the machine. "You seeing Roger again tonight?"

"Maybe. You seeing Kevin?"

Sarah winces. "No. He stood me up at dinner a couple nights ago. Again."

"He's been doing a lot of that, lately." Now Annette bends to poke at the place where the pictures should come out. "Maybe it's an occupational hazard. No one can get a cable guy to show up when he's supposed to."

Sarah smiles, but it fades, and she nibbles her bottom lip. "Well, we're sort of off for now."

Annette puts her hand on Sarah's shoulder. "Are you okay?"

Sarah nods. "Yeah. I'm okay."

"Hey, look!" Annette points to the black and white strip of photos that have gotten stuck halfway out of the machine. "There they are. Sort of." She tugs at them, but they don't give.

Sarah reaches to lend a hand, but pauses. She looks over her shoulder, eyes searching again as though she senses being watched. Her gaze brushes over me, and I feel it as a tickle of air across my face. I get goosebumps.

"Ha!" Annette straightens, holding up the photos in triumph. She spots Sarah's expression, and frowns.

"What's up?" She looks, too, at the sea of passing faces.

"I don't know. Just a weird feeling." Then she shakes her head, and reaches for the pictures. "Let's see if they fit the locket." She smiles.

The scene faded to the blackness of my closed eyelids. Nausea swept over me again, and I sucked in a breath. Sounds of the city street swelled in my ears. I stumbled back, and as my hand came out of Annette's pocket, I felt a cool oval of metal in my hand.

"Mick? You all right?" Annette urged me toward my apartment building. "You're pale."

I opened my hand and showed her the locket. As I climbed the steps, I pried it open. Inside, a black and white photo of two sisters stared back at me, both with silly, cross-eyed smiles.

"You saw her again, didn't you?" Annette took the locket. "I didn't do that on purpose. I swear."

My head was still reeling. The tip of my nose felt numb, like I'd had a gallon of wine. "How did you know I could see your sister if I touched something of hers?"

She slipped the locket inside her coat, and looked far off down the street.

"Annette." I took her shoulders. "You're the only one that's ever figured it out. What are you not telling me?"

She pulled from my hands, and frowned.

"Fine. I didn't want anything to do with this, anyway." I climbed the apartment steps, and shoved my key into the lock on the wrought iron door.

"Okay," she said. She came to stand behind me. "You're not the first person I've known who could see things. Except this other person never saw things that already happened. She saw things that hadn't happened yet, and spent her life feeling crazy for it."

I turned to face her. "You mean Sarah."

She nodded. She hugged the collar of her jacket against her throat. "She'd see things as though she were standing in the room, watching. Most of the time, she didn't have enough information to find the people in her visions to warn them, but she'd read about them in the paper after, or see them on the news." She sighed. "She used to say what you did. That if she couldn't stop it from happening, she wasn't really helping anyone." She closed her eyes. "In the end, she couldn't even help herself."

"You think she knew she was going to die?" I asked.

She nodded. "I think she knew. That night, we were supposed to go to a party, but she called to say she didn't think she should. She sounded scared. She said she was going to stay home with the doors locked, and that she'd call me in the morning."

I watched her eyes as they filled with tears, then had to look away. After a time, I pushed open the apartment doors. "Come on upstairs. I've got beer, I think."

"So you're going to help me?"

I shook my head. "I don't know how much help I'll be, but I think I was involved before you ever asked."

Her brow wrinkled. "What do you mean?"

I held the door open, and waved her in. "Remember you told me she kept getting the feeling she was being followed? Watched by some guy? Something like that?"

"Yeah." She eyed me as she stepped inside.

"I think that guy was me."

§

In my apartment, I pried the lid off a Michelob left over from Rog's beer donation, and offered it to Annette.

She gulped twice, then pressed the back of her hand to her mouth. "Now explain yourself."

I snapped open a can of Bud Light. "I'm not sure I can. I don't get it, myself."

"Then what makes you think you're the guy?"

I shook my head. "I don't know. It's stupid, I guess."

"No, you said it for a reason. What are you thinking?"

"It's more a feeling. I mean, usually when I shift, I'm a part of the scene, but I'm a ghost." I slumped onto the couch. "Both times when I saw your sister, she reacted. She didn't see me or anything, but when she looked around, it felt like she was looking for me."

Annette set down her Michelob and slid onto the couch beside me. "How is that possible? You think it has something to do with her own ability?"

I shrugged. I sucked at my can.

"I'll pay whatever you normally charge for investigating, plus expenses. Plus, whatever else you want," she said.

I lowered my drink and regarded her.

Her blue eyes stared hard at my face, pleading. "I know it won't bring her back, but I've got to see that bastard pay for what he did. You must know how that feels."

"What if what I see doesn't help you?"

She turned and looked out across the room. "At least I'll know I turned over every rock." She opened her purse. She rummaged through it, lifted a small chain, and offered it toward me. A gold key dangled against the back of my hand. "Take it. It's to her apartment."

"Her apartment?"

Her lips pressed into a flat line. "I've been paying the rent so I can keep it just the way it was that night. I don't know why, exactly. Maybe… to always remember. Maybe in case the police ever need to come back." She sighed. "I know it's crazy."

I was quiet for a moment, watching her. Then I shook my head. "It's not crazy."

I took the key.

§

I stood at the doorway of Sarah's apartment. Frayed bits of yellow police tape were still stapled to the frame. The door handle and lock were new, obnoxiously shiny against the backdrop of warped, peeling wood. I turned the key. I pushed open the door.

A window at the far end dimly lighted the hallway.

From what I could see, one end of a curtain rod was yanked from the wall, and the curtain drooped to the floor. A door was ajar to a room on the left, and when I leaned that way, I could see the corner of a wrought-iron bed through the crack.

I didn't want to go in. I'd be walking on carpet where she'd walked. I'd be looking into mirrors that had reflected her face. No matter how many times I'd done this before, I'd always felt as though I was invading their privacy. I felt like that now. Not to mention that my shifts tended to control me, instead of the other way around, and I was never sure what would set one off, or what I'd be seeing when I got there.

I took my first step. Nothing dramatic happened, so I shoved my hands into my pockets, and kept walking. I reached the door on the left, and nudged it open with my shoulder.

Her bedroom. The wrought-iron bed was massive, and took up nearly the entire floor space. A quilt stitched with pastels in a wedding ring pattern was rumpled against the foot of the bed. An antique dressing table squatted in the left corner of the room, draped with hair ribbons and colorful glass bottles. A short metal stand to the right held hand weights.

I moved down the hall. It opened into the main room, which blended into the kitchen. Around the entire room, frameless paintings were torn and scattered. Artist brushes, some caked with dried paint, some clean but snapped in pieces, littered the mess. Black smears like ghostly tentacles clung to tabletops, edges of paintings, and some broken brushes. The police had done a thorough search for fingerprints.

I followed the trail of brushes to a cabinet against the wall. Inside, the cabinet was crammed with more brushes, tubes of artist tints, and some blank canvases. Her easel was folded and leaned in a corner.

I moved into the kitchen, separated from the main room by a low counter. Dishes were piled in the sink, but they looked clean. More dishes lined a wooden drying rack on top of a gingham dishcloth.

Another door off the main room led to the bathroom. A quick peek inside showed a pink towel over the shower curtain rod, a fluffy toilet seat cover, and more black smudges around the sink. So far, nothing set off a shift, but I hadn't touched anything, either.

I worked my way back through the main room. The way the paintings had been destroyed, either before the murder, or after, personalized the violence.

Sarah's attacker knew her, and wanted to destroy her so completely that he couldn't even leave her paintings intact. So how did she know him?

I came to her bedroom again. I stood for a while in the doorway, deciding what to touch, and then working up my nerve to do it. A person spends so much time in their bed, I was sure to make a connection there. I inched toward it, and rested my hand on a fat knot of metal on her footboard. I felt my stomach twitch.

I'm standing in her bedroom. I think it's night, because the windows are dark, and the room is full of shadows.

A tiffany lamp lookalike casts faint, colored light from her dressing table. Quietly filtering from the next room is Tchaikovsky's *The Sleeping Beauty* ballet. The acrid smell of burned food is in the air.

She must have failed at whatever she recently tried to make.

I think it's cookies. As my eyes adjust, I see her move across the room.

She stands in front of the tall mirror of the table. Her hair is up in a ponytail, but damp around her face like she's just out of a shower. She's wearing a long tank top that stops at the top of her thighs, and thick, pink slippers.

My eyes trail the delicate curve of her throat, and the dip of her skin at her collarbone.

She frowns at her reflection, but I can't see why she's disappointed. She leans in and presses the skin around her eyes. She turns her head a little. She pushes at her forehead, smoothing lines I can't see, then she lowers her hands. "Well. You've still got brains, at least," she tells herself. Then she sticks out her tongue.

She moves away from the mirror and stops. Her eyes scan the room, and then narrow. She spins to face the doorway. "Is someone in here? Kevin?" She's not answered. She reaches for a hand weight from the rack and holds it like a baseball bat. She stalks out of the room.

I hear the front door chain rattle. She's testing it. She passes the doorway, her weight gripped high.

Tchaikovsky is clicked off. The bathroom door creaks open. Her slippers scuffle back across the carpet, and she is again in the bedroom, hand on her hip, perplexed. But she shakes her head and replaces the hand weight.

Then she turns, very slowly. Her dark eyes focus at the foot of the bed where I'm standing. I startle. Then I remember she isn't really seeing me, but looking right through me. I feel conspicuous anyway.

"Is someone there?" she asks in a whisper.

"Yes," I say, surprised at my own voice.

She doesn't hear me. She searches the air with her hand, and it passes right through me. Then she makes a frightened little sound, and touches her hand to her head. "Sarah Caldwell, you are losing your mind," she says.

I can tell by her expression she's not convinced. She continues to stare through me, and pulls in a deep breath, lifting her chest. She eases toward the foot of the bed. For some reason, I back up.

Her fingers tremble as she reaches to touch the curve of metal at the bedpost. Just before contact, she pulls them back, and frowns. Slowly, her eyes turn to rest on the knot of metal under my hand. She inches forward again.

I'm terrified and fascinated at the same time. I want to let go, but she's standing right in front of me, smelling of Ivory soap. A loose strand of her hair tickles my chin. She's staring hard at my hand, her breath shallow and quick. I see the throb of her pulse in her neck. My pulse is racing, too.

Her hand reaches again, hesitates, and then grips the metal under my hand. Then her fingers are on my hand. She sucks in a squeak of air and lifts her chin. Our eyes meet. She sees me. For a moment, all of time is suspended while we stare at each other, breath held. Then she moans and spins away to run for the door.

"Sarah!" I yell, and chase after her.

I ran through the bedroom doorway so fast that I slammed against the wall of the hallway. Dazed, I turned to follow her into the main room. "Sarah, wait!"

She wasn't there. A snap under my shoe made me look down. I'd broken a green-handled brush. An old, dried brush that reminded me I'd been seeing her past, and that here in the present, Sarah was dead.

I fell to my knees and hugged my churning stomach. She was dead, but not for that brief moment she looked into my eyes. Somehow, I'd reached into her world, or she'd reached into mine. We'd touched. If she could touch me, she could hear me. Somehow, I had to make her hear me.

My fingers found the broken wood of her artist brush. I fought against the surge of nausea and gripped it tightly.

I'm kneeling in her main room. The lace curtains are open and sunlight streams through the dusty windows. She's sitting on a barstool, feet pulled up, balancing her heels and her backside on the small, vinyl seat. One arm hugs her legs, and the other is sweeping strokes across a canvas perched on an easel.

Her hand stops. She looks down. Her eyes glance toward me, then she puts her brush to canvas again, and continues, but her brow is wrinkled.

I push to my feet. I move closer, and try speaking. "Sarah, don't be afraid."

She doesn't respond, but her hand stops again, and sets the brush down. "Are you here?" she asks, and looks to where I'd been kneeling.

Standing behind her, I see what she's painting. A face. My face. I stumble back.

She slides off the stool and talks toward the floor. "Look, I don't know what's going on, but it's really freaking me out, and I wish you'd stop. Maybe it's supposed to be funny or something. It isn't." She nudges a toe at the carpet. "Did you hear me? Go away."

I stay. I stare at my face on the canvas. It isn't finished, but I recognize my eyes, and the jut of my chin. I'm wearing a red Old Navy shirt in the portrait, like I'm wearing now. It looks just like me, even without my hair painted in. She's good. Really good.

She throws a sheet over the easel, covering the painting. She glares through me. "Are you a ghost?"

The Ghost of Christmas Past, I want to say.

There's a long silence. She nibbles her lip. Her eyes turn toward her windowsill, where a glass jar holds multi-colored brushes. I think she's looking at the green-handled one.

Her doorbell rings. She startles. She looks toward the door, toward me. Then she huffs and disappears around the corner. "What the? What's he doing here?" Her voice is muffled, like she's talking against the door.

I hear the door swing open.

"Kevin? What are you doing here?"

The floor swayed, and I gripped the counter as I went dizzy. My stomach wrenched. I gulped air. No good. I lurched into the bathroom, dropped to my knees at the toilet, and threw up.

I'd gone forward in her time. My shifts usually skipped around, depending on what I was touching, and they rarely made sense strung together. The shifts with Sarah felt different. I recognized that each time I saw her, I was getting closer and closer to the time she died. If I didn't touch the right object, would I miss my chance?

I arched toward the toilet and threw up again. Sweat broke out across my forehead. I felt hot and cold at the same time. Somehow, my body was suffering, more than it had ever reacted before.

I had to get my bearings before I tried again. I rested my forehead against the cool porcelain.

The shower turned itself on.

I'm kneeling at the toilet, watching steam rise above the plastic shower curtain beside me. She's singing "You're So Vain." Carly Simon has no competition, but I think Sarah knows, and enjoys singing anyway. I can see the faint shadow of her curves through the curtain, and she's holding a back brush to her mouth like a microphone. I smile, despite my aching head.

Her song stops.

"You are kidding me!" she hollers. "What are you, some sort of pervert ghost?"

The back brush sails over the top of the shower curtain, and passes through me to land in the toilet. "Get out of here! Leave me alone!"

Her hand reaches out, patting for her pink towel. The towel disappears into the shower, and when the water turns off, she hops out and barrels past, wrapped in pink. "Did you hear me? Leave me alone!" She slams the bathroom door behind herself.

I dry heaved at the toilet. I spasmed. I felt like I was coming apart from the inside out. I had to get out of this apartment before it killed me. I tried to stand, but my legs felt like rubber. I had to crawl to the door. My hand shook on the knob. Hadn't I left it open?

I yanked the door, and fell onto the carpet on the other side. The shag scratched my cheek, and smelled like burned cookies. I grabbed at the leg of the sofa to haul myself forward, but couldn't move. I just had to rest for a minute. I just had to think.

"I'm not ready yet," I hear her say. Then she screams. I look up from where I'm laying on the floor to see her staring at me. She's perched on the arm of the sofa, a phone in her hand. She drops the phone, and leaps to her feet.

Her towel comes loose, and she catches it, and

tucks the end in itself.

"Sarah?" asks a voice inside the phone. "Sarah, what's going on?"

She watches toward me and bends to pick up the phone. Her hand is trembling. "I'm here." She swallows hard. "I just thought I saw a… a cockroach. It's gone, though. Or I was imagining it, I don't know. I'm having a weird night." She walks toward me and pokes her foot toward my shoulder.

I don't feel it.

"No, you go on ahead," she says. "I'll meet you there. I'm going to be so late." She kneels, and then passes her hand through my head. "Hey, Annette? Do you believe in ghosts?" She sits back on her heels. "Well, if you did, do you think they stick around for a reason? I mean, do you suppose they're trying to tell someone something?" She stands and turns the corner into the hall.

I can still hear her talking.

"You know, on second thought, I'm not really in the mood for a party tonight. There's something bizarre going on here, and I'm going to lock myself in until I figure it out."

I groan. I realize she's talking about the party that she never goes to. I know tonight is the night she dies, because she stays home. And now I wonder if, somehow, it's all because of me.

The suspicion only makes me suffer more. Already, each minute that passes becomes more painful. The carpet scratches like steel wool on my cheek, and I can barely keep my grip on the sofa leg. But I hang on, because I must. I must.

She comes into the room again, dressed in jeans with holes in the knees, and a pink tee shirt. Her wet hair dribbles water down her chest. She draws her bottom lip between her teeth. Then she touches the arm of the sofa.

She gasps. She draws back her hand.

Tentatively, she tries again. This time, she doesn't run. She looks right at me. "Who are you? How do you keep getting in here?"

"Get out," I try to say through my throat choked with gravel.

"Are you sick?" She climbs onto the sofa on her knees, and crawls toward me. "Is that how you died?"

"Not a ghost," I say, and turn my head to see her better. The motion sends a blast of pain down my spine.

"Then what are you?" She leans over the edge of the cushion, and touches my face. Her fingers are cool, and they feel good. "You're burning up. You are sick."

"Listen," I croak. "Get out. Right now."

She shakes her head. "No. I want to help you, so you can go on to the great beyond, or whatever, and leave me alone."

"Not a ghost," I say again. My jaw clenches. I'm having hard time speaking.

"But you are trying to tell me something."

Pain slices into my gut, and I grunt. I convulse.

"No!" I shouted, feeling my hand jerk away from

the sofa leg. Not yet. Not now. I tried to grab the sofa again, but my body wouldn't let me. I thrashed, feeling the carpet slice into my face, my hands. I felt like I was dying.

My body went rigid, but at least I wasn't thrashing anymore. I was on my back now, and I stared up at the ceiling, trying to focus. I could move one inch at a time that way, staring hard and concentrating. Twist the shoulders, scoot the feet. It was my chance to creep for the door.

I stopped. If I left now, Sarah would die. Or, she was already dead, so the only person I could save now was me. I didn't know which was the truth. I didn't know what I was fighting for.

Just then, something pressed into my side.

I roll over to find Sarah pushing a rubber spatula against my ribs. "There you are," she says.

I grip the plastic. "Spatula?" I ask, blinking, trying to figure out how she found me.

"It was the first thing I grabbed. I can see you when we both touch the same thing."

The shifts happen so fast I don't even see them coming. I'm still trying to orient. I try to sit up. Maybe if I can get my head level, it will stop spinning.

Sarah holds the other end of the spatula, and tries to help me.

I reach with my free hand for something to boost me up. I feel cloth, and yank. I hear a curtain rod come out of the plaster, and lace drops over my face.

"Whoa, look out. You're going to hurt yourself," she says.

"You have to get out of here," I say.

Hot pain claws inside me again.

I jerk, and feel the spatula coming out of my hand. I clutch at the air, trying to keep Sarah near. I grab her shirt. I feel it in my hand, bunched against my palm.

She says something I can't understand. She sounds scared.

I double over, and vomit on her carpet. This time it's not dry, it's blood.

She fades away, then comes back, fades away, and then comes back. Her hands try to help me, but pass right through me.

I clutch the fabric of her shirt even tighter. I must convince her to leave. Now.

I try the first thing that comes into my head. I dip my hand into my blood, and write a message, the only message I can think of that will send her out without a second thought.

She fades again and doesn't come back.

I dropped hard on my face.

A broken paintbrush stabbed me in the side, and I didn't have the strength to move it. Light faded around my eyes like I was being sucked into a tunnel, and the last thing I saw was my own bloody message scrawled on the carpet: ANNETTE.

Everything went black.

§

My cell phone blasted its rendition of Beethoven's Fifth.

I let it get to the reprise before I flopped off the couch and crawled to where the phone was clipped to my jeans, left in a pile where I slid them off last night. I checked the caller ID. Rog. I almost didn't answer.

"Yeah?" I said into the phone.

"Mick, are you sleeping? What's the deal? It's three o'clock."

"So?" I looked at my wrist, but I wasn't wearing a watch. Suddenly I was gripped by déjà vu. A headache, like the mother of all hangovers, surged behind my eyes. I leaned back against the couch, and tried to think around the pain.

"So I've been calling you for hours. It was a wild night last night. You're going to want to know all about it."

"Wild night?" I asked. Concentrating only made my head worse, and the patches of fog in my mind refused to pull into a memory.

"What's up? Are you drunk?" Roger asked.

I ran my hand through my hair. "No. Maybe. I've got a jackhammer in my head, and I don't remember getting home last night."

"Just like old times, man. But you've got to guzzle some coffee and pull yourself together. Meet me at Buford's in 10 minutes."

"Why?" I asked, not sure I wanted to bother getting

dressed.

"They arrested the guy that killed Dee."

I was on my feet. "Make it five."

"Don't scrimp. You need time to brush your teeth, because you'll be meeting someone important to me."

"Five minutes, Rog." I closed the phone. I grabbed my jeans. I splashed some water on my face, ran my wet hands through my hair, and tugged a shirt over my head as I closed the apartment door behind me.

I made it outside, and realized I'd forgotten my jacket. Cool air crept right through my cotton shirt, and I tucked my hands under my armpits. No matter. I was a man on a mission. I dodged cars, jumped to avoid a kid on a skateboard, and finally made it to the door of my sandwich shop.

Roger was there, smiling at me, his arms crossed. "You look cold."

"I am. Tell me about last night."

"Let's get a seat."

We moved to the back of the shop, and Roger ordered some iced tea. I wanted a beer, but settled for water.

"Well?" I said, once we were settled.

"The cops tried to call you last night, too, but you wouldn't pick up. The guy that killed Dee was Kevin Lanford, your cable guy."

"Kevin. The cable guy." A shiver crept my spine.

"You described him to a tee. The cops suspected him all along. They knew he'd been there earlier that day, but forensics couldn't put him on the scene at the time of death."

"They told me that four years ago."

"Yeah, well. Last night he confessed. Seems Dee wasn't the only one, either. Cops said once the guy got bragging, he wouldn't shut up."

I shook my head. It hardly seemed real, after all this time. "How do you know all this?"

Roger opened a packet of sugar into his iced tea. "That's the wild part. Hold on to your chair, man."

"I'm holding."

"Okay, last night I get a call from my girlfriend, Annette. She's who you're going to meet today, by the way. I hadn't really said anything to you about her, because I didn't want to jinx anything. You know how I am."

"Annette Caldwell?"

"Yeah." Roger blinked. "You know her?"

"Well, don't I? I mean, didn't I meet her already or something?"

"Nah, I don't think so. I was waiting to tell you about her once I was sure."

"Sure about what?"

"That she's the one, Mick." He leaned back, and gave me a wide, cheesy grin.

I smiled, too. "That's great, Rog. Really." I shifted in my chair. "But about last night?"

"Oh yeah. Okay, so I get this call, right? And it's Annette, and she's at the Fifth Precinct, and could I come pick her up? So, when I get there, I find out Annette was at a party when her sister showed up, all freaked out about seeing a ghost or something, telling her Annette was in trouble."

"Sarah?"

"Yeah, you know her, too?"

Wispy patches of brain fog were beginning to clear, but what I was trying to get hold of was still deep and irritating, like an unreachable itch. "Maybe. I think so."

"Well, of course Annette was fine, but her sister was such a basket case that Annette took her home. When they got to her apartment, they found Sarah's old boyfriend trashing the place. Guess who he was."

I felt my face go cold. "Kevin."

"Give the man a Bozo button," said Roger. "He still had a key to the apartment, I guess, and let himself in. He found some painting of a guy Sarah had been working on, and thought he was the one she broke up with him over, something like that. He gave Annette a black eye, and he broke Sarah's arm before Annette clocked him with a frying pan." Roger made a fist. "She's tough."

"Yeah," I said. "Major cojones."

"Are you guys talking about me?" Annette appeared at the table and crossed her arms. She was wearing a blue sweater that turned her eyes a bright sapphire and lit up the swollen bruise on her cheekbone.

Roger stood up and slid his arm around Annette's waist. "I was just telling him how you nailed that guy with a frying pan."

Annette nodded. "I keep thinking about what might have happened if I hadn't been there with Sarah."

"So do I," came a voice behind Annette.

Now I stood.

Sarah peered brown eyes around her sister's shoulder, and my breath caught. She was so beautiful. Like her sister, only softer. Like my Dee, only younger. For a moment, all of time suspended while we stared at each other, breath held.

Memories that I'd been scrabbling for blasted at me like a movie on fast forward.

I reeled, and had to grab the back of my chair.

Sarah stepped closer to me. Her right arm was in a sling, and her left held something behind her back. "The police let me in my apartment to get this. I thought you should see it." From behind her back, she withdrew a portrait.

I stared at my face on the canvas.

It wasn't finished, but I recognized my eyes and the jut of my chin. I wore a red Old Navy shirt in the portrait, like I was wearing now. It looked just like me, even without my hair painted in.

"You're good," I said. "Really good."

"I had to tape it together. It's all messy in the back." She flipped the canvas around to show me how she puzzled the parts back together with duct tape. "Once my arm's better, I was thinking I'd try again."

"Uh, how have you two met before?" Roger asked.

I turned to find he and Annette staring at the two of us like we'd sprouted dandelions on our heads.

"Actually," said Sarah. "I was hoping Mick could tell me that." She smiled up at my face.

My headache disappeared. I smiled, too. "Come on up to my apartment. I think I have beer."

MAY I HAVE THIS

Strangers pass without looking

casting shadows at their feet

dancing

for a moment

as friends who long to meet

BEAUTY MARK

"It's ugly," she says, and presses her knuckles together, buried beneath chenille.

"Not ugly," I say, and crawl my fingers along the front of her robe, trying to open it again.

She regards me, storm clouds gathering across her face.

"I love you," I say. "Everything about you."

She turns her back, staring instead out the window. Her face hovers, ghost-like, in the pane, and her eyes are hollow shadows filling with tears.

"I want to see it."

She peeks at me over her shoulder, and I raise my brows, smiling. She faces me, her jaw tight. But she draws open her robe, just a little, to let me see.

My hands are rough. I'm careful to touch gently. And I'm spellbound as my finger follows the

shimmering trail, like snail shine across a moonlit leaf,
of the stretch mark on her growing belly.

DADE'S SPECIAL LEMON

Herbert once complained there weren't enough libraries at Disney World. He also criticized clowns for garish cosmetics, handmade quilts for uneven stitching, and rainbows for lack of color theme.

I hadn't gotten to know Herbert very well by the time he commented on my denim skirt. "Too casual for the office," he'd said. After that I only wore it on weekends. It shouldn't have mattered, he wasn't my boss, but Herbert had a way of talking down to even the tallest person in the room.

I was an easy target, I suppose. I spent most of my time feeling pretty small. Trying to keep it that way.

I was wearing that denim skirt Saturday night. I'd been driving home from a late, ordinary dinner, and had taken a left turn at Market Street to discover, of all things, a carnival.

Only yesterday, that dusty plot had a single, drooping maple tree; suddenly it was cramped with creaking rides and squealing children.

I'd found my car veering toward the parking lot without me really thinking about it. Now I sat with the motor running, watching giant, mildewed teacups whirl around a rusted platform. The smell of hot grease wafted through my open car window.

I didn't even know why I was here. I hated carnivals. Especially the made-in-a-weekend kind that filled neighborhoods with even more sounds of everyone having fun but me.

Except for carousels. I loved old, weathered horses and the wild animals of the merry-go-rounds of yesteryear.

I finally realized that's what I was doing here. I was curious if the place had a merry-go-round.

I turned off my motor and got out. I circled behind the teacups and the midway tents, and then heard the sound of organ music. I followed it.

There it was. It was as faded and aged as I'd expected, but I wasn't disappointed. In fact, I pulled my cell phone from the pocket of my denim skirt to take a picture.

That's when I met the hunched little man who was running it. I didn't notice him right away; I was focusing on the peeling paint of a wood lion. But he commented on my shoes.

"I'm sorry?" I said and leaned over a little to hear him better.

"I like your shoes," he repeated. "Sensible kind. They match your pretty skirt."

At first, I thought he was teasing. Then I wondered if he was flirting.

He grinned up at me, tipping his head because he couldn't straighten his back. His eyes had a kind of light behind them, but it may have been a reflection of the merry-go-round's canopy bulbs.

I was still regarding the hunchback, trying to read his expression, when I was suddenly bumped into from behind. "Watch yourself there, Justine."

I immediately knew who it was; I recognized his whiny voice. Herbert. I managed to turn and look at him without groaning.

Herbert's arms hung awkwardly at his sides. "Funny, us meeting like this. I was on my way home, and the lights attracted me." Herbert pointed at the top of the carousel, at a broken shaft. "Flag's missing."

"Yes," I said.

"Fourteen lights burned out, and the unicorn's not pumping up and down."

"I like the lion," I said.

Herbert's head bobbled in a lopsided nod. "Are you going to ride it in that skirt? Awfully dressy for a carnival, isn't it?"

I didn't owe him an explanation, but I gave one anyway. "No, I don't ride carousels."

When he stared at me, unblinking, I found myself trying even harder to explain. "I hadn't planned on stopping, either. The lights attracted me, too, I guess."

"And cotton candy," said the hunchbacked worker, where he stood beside Herbert. "I'll bet you haven't had any since you were a kid."

I smiled at him, grateful for his conversational help. "There is something special about cotton candy."

"Wait until you try ours." The man's eyes still held that backlight.

"Just sugar and air," said Herbert.

"Well," I said. "I'm going to get some. Excuse me, gentlemen."

"Tell them to give you Dade's Special Lemon." The hunched man winked.

I nodded and ducked away. I hoped, expected, it was the last I'd see of Herbert that night, but by the time I wound my way along paths of beaten grass between rides and people to reach the metal confectionary trailer, Herbert was leaning against it, waiting beneath painted pink and yellow words reading *Cotton Candy. Honest Goodness.* He had his arms crossed, and he was scowling the way he did when he was gearing up to reprimand my choice of jewelry as a professional representative of Caullingworth Insurance.

"The shortest distance, Justine. Point A to point B."

"I hadn't realized you were joining me," I said, trying not to grit my teeth.

Herbert leaned toward the girl behind the window. "We'd like cotton candy, please. Dade's Special Lemon. Just one." Then, over his shoulder, he asked me, "You don't mind sharing, right?"

It didn't seem to matter whether or not I did.

He opened the bag when it came and offered out the citrus-yellow fluff. "Funny us meeting here like this, isn't it?" he said again.

I plucked a pinch of sugar and put it in my mouth. It dissolved instantly, the tang nipping the sides of my tongue.

In that moment, I was drawn back to my last carnival, walking with my dad toward the Jumbo Whirl. I was fourteen, all gawk, with limp braids and plaid gaucho pants. I'd passed the merry-go-round, wistfully longing to ride, but I'd already spent the half hour drive there listening to my father's tirade about how merry-go-rounds were for babies, and that I'd be riding his dad-approved rides, or I'd have to walk home. I'd paused, just briefly, to watch a little hunched man unhook the line to let people on. Do they do always assign hunchbacks to the merry-go-round? Then I'd dutifully followed my father to his ride of choice, instead.

I hated the Jumbo Whirl.

"I threw up. Twice," I said.

Herbert stopped chewing his bite of cotton candy and blinked.

"Last time I came to a carnival. It got all over Josh Kramer's shoes. The basketball captain." Weird. I hadn't told anyone that before.

"Oh."

I reached for more candy.

"I've never even been to a carnival," said Herbert.

My hand paused. "Ever?"

He shook his head. "My mother warned me of

low maintenance rides and high prices for poor-quality food."

"She probably has a point."

Herbert nodded. He ate another bite of candy, and so did I. "This tastes delicious," he said.

I had to agree. It may have been just sugar and air, but it was satisfying like a meal, and I felt stronger. Taller, somehow.

"I saw your car in the parking lot," blurted Herbert. "I recognized the patch of rust on your bumper. Plus, I have your license plate memorized."

Now I stopped chewing to stare. Even I didn't know my plate number.

"Not in a creepy way," said Herbert. "At least, not on purpose. I have eidetic memory."

"Oh," I said. I reached for more candy, and Herbert stepped forward with the bag.

"It's why I came in," he said. "I sat for a while, wondering what all the fuss was about. Then I saw your car, and I suddenly wanted to see you."

I took a moment to process. Then, I meant to reply with a generic, polite sort of acknowledgement, but what came out was, "I had to consciously restrain myself from grimacing when I saw you."

Herbert winced. "I'm not surprised."

"You're not?"

He shook his head and looked off toward the Spider Swing.

Again, I tried to give one of my usual reassurances, the way I often tried to smooth uncomfortable situations. Instead, I said, "I have to sacrifice too much of my own self just to get along with you."

He looked back at me, his dark eyes encircled by sad shadows. "I wish it didn't have to be that way."

"Me too," I said.

"It's like how some people have an extra rod in their eyes to see more colors on the spectrum. I can see more flaws."

He offered out the bag, and my eyes scanned the brightly printed, yellow-and-pink letters of *Dade's Special Lemon Cotton Candy. Honest Goodness.*

I said, "You see more anomalies. It doesn't make them flaws."

Herbert went still and looked up from our hands into my face. He blinked once. Then he gripped my hand and gently led me over fat, bunched electric cords, muddied popcorn kernels, and discarded corndog sticks. He drew me away from the crowd, and we ducked behind a faded Port-A-Potty.

"Justine," he said, "Would you let me kiss you?"

"You want to kiss me?"

He nodded, his gaze settling onto my mouth.

"Why?" I asked.

He pulled back a little, took in a deep breath. "Because you stopped wearing your denim skirt to the office, and you switched perfumes so I would stop sneezing, and, after all this time, you still try not to grimace at me when we talk."

I considered. "Well, I'm not attracted to you, but it's been a long time since anyone asked to kiss me, so

I'd like to at least remember what one is like."

He smiled. He touched his fingertips to my cheek. Then he leaned in and pressed his lips to mine.

The kiss was warm and dry, and tasted like lemon.

Just then, the Port-A-Potty lurched awkwardly, sending me off-balance and breaking the kiss. I clutched Herbert's arm to steady myself.

The potty door swung open. Out hobbled the hunched little carnival worker. "Oh!" he said, looking up, askew. "Hello, again."

I glanced at Herbert. His cheeks were blotchy with blush.

"How's that Dade's Special Lemon?" asked the man, nodding toward the bag in Herbert's hand.

"Delicious," we both said.

"Oh, good." He rubbed his knobby hands together. "Well, back to work. You two ride the Jumbo Whirl yet?"

"Oh, no," I said, holding up my hand. "Never again."

"Ah, that's right," He winked. "See you in line." He lumbered off.

I looked back at Herbert. He was scowling down at the mud on his shoes. "Herbert," I said. "I'm going to stay a little longer."

"All right. I'm going to take off," he said. "Got an early tee time in the morning."

"I'll see you Monday, then." I pointed to the bag of cotton candy. "Are you going to finish that?"

Herbert shook his head and passed the bag into

my hand. Then he took a step back but paused. "Is this going to be awkward? Monday?"

I laughed. "Yes."

He opened his mouth to speak, closed it, and then gave a smile and a brief wave. I hadn't seen him smile before, that I could remember. Turned out, it was a nice one. He turned and headed for the parking lot.

I watched him for a few steps, my hand coming to rest on my mouth, remembering. Then I turned, too, and got in line for the merry-go-round.

OUT

Blossoming

from the inside out, you're

soaking up sun

instead of resisting

feeding your soul

instead of subsisting

claiming your space

instead of existing

it takes time for your world,

your skin,

to change, but

on the inside

you're out

THE DREAMCATCHER BRIDGE

Angela awoke from the sound of drums in her dreams. She lay on the ground, on her sleeping bag gone damp from the earth below it and her body atop it. She was crying.

"Are you awake?" asked Caleb, who shifted in the dark beside her. He sat up, a troll silhouette against the wall of their tent.

"Mm-hmm." She pushed at her tears with the heels of her hands.

"I haven't slept all night," said Caleb.

Angela hadn't slept all week. Not really. Since the memorial service, there had been dishes to wash, houseguests to feed, and sympathy cards to read and reply to. She'd been busy seeing to the details of paperwork and legalities. Whenever she had laid in bed, she'd closed her eyes, but rest hadn't come; only drums beating incessantly in her dreams, hollow and distant and somehow frightening.

Her last words to her brother, Rob, had been shouted at him in the garage, over the sound of him banging on his acoustic set; the same set he'd been promising for a year to move out of the way to make room for her elliptical trainer. He'd called her selfish. She'd called him an infant.

"We'll be there tomorrow," said Caleb. By the tightness of his voice, Angela guessed he'd been crying too.

§

Morning came, breathing lilac. Angela stared at a patch of the wild blossoms, listening to the clank of tent poles while Caleb cleared the campsite. "I haven't been here in so long," she said. "I'd forgotten them."

Caleb paused. He came to stand beside her, his hand on her back. "We liked to celebrate our anniversary here," said Caleb. "Just so he could cut a branch to take back."

"You always managed to be here when they were in bloom," said Angela. "Even now."

Caleb retrieved his pocketknife and sliced off the end of a blossom-covered branch. "Even now."

By afternoon, they trudged in silence. Angela felt the sun on her shoulders like a boulder; it grew heavier as it rose higher, making each step a struggle. Even Caleb's breathing was strained. The straps of his backpack stained his shirt gray. He paused to shift his pack.

Angela took the moment to rummage for a water bottle. "Are we lost?"

Caleb frowned. "I know the way."

She wasn't sure. "The forest has changed a lot."

He dragged his wrist across his forehead. "Not so much." But he looked up and around at the trees, studying them like strangers.

A dragonfly swooped past Angela's cheek. She watched the bounce of its powder blue body and the way the sunlight glistened the veins in its transparent wings. It circled her waist and then landed on a shaft of feathery grass. It swayed, its head tilted, grinning.

She moved closer, and it lifted again to the air, only to land once more a few yards away. She followed it.

"Where are you going?" Caleb called.

"I think it's this way. I hear frogs." And she did. Water was near. She hurried, trampling soft undergrowth, feeling tree roots like knuckles beneath her boots.

Then they were there. Before them swung the suspension bridge of their youth, as shambling and faded as Angela remembered.

"Why do you think he chose here?" asked Caleb, behind her.

She didn't know. "I would have picked differently."

She stepped onto a disintegrating plank. She flexed, testing. Then she moved on, easing her way to the middle of the structure, watching the shallow flow of water beneath her feet smoothing tiny river stones. When Caleb joined her, she lowered her backpack from her shoulders and reached inside it for a metal box.

"Should we say something?" Caleb asked.

"I think it's all been said." At the service; at the wake; at the door as mourners came and went. Angela was empty of words.

She pushed the box through the suspension wires, met Caleb's eyes, and then released her brother's ashes into the water below.

"Wait," said Caleb. He withdrew the crumpled lilac branch from his backpack and tossed it over the side. It caught on a rock and gathered ashes against its lavender blossoms. The powder blue dragonfly flitted down to a leaf, its head tilted, grinning. Then the branch broke loose, and lilac, ashes and dragonfly drifted lazily away.

"I loved him," said Caleb, and took Angela's hand.

"So did I," she said.

§

They made camp that night near the brook. Angela lay on her side, listening to the ripple of water, hearing the memory of her brother's voice within it. Singing, not shouting. Gentle rhythms, not banging drums. She closed her eyes.

"I think Rob is happy," said Caleb into the darkness.

"Yes," said Angela. She released a breath, and then dreamlessly slept.

MEDA'S CLEARING

Meda Lillin's hands are bent around the handles of her rocking chair. Her knuckles are brown and knobby like the wood beneath them, and I have to peer closely to see where the rocking chair ends and her skin begins. She's smiling, and staring out through the window, and she's very still. Her rocking chair works, but she doesn't use it that way.

Her cotton dress sweeps down her bony legs and puddles around yellow sandals that used to be white. The shoes expose toenails that are thick and too long and meticulously polished to match the pink petals where the sandals fasten.

Meda's room is as still as she is. The window is open, but there's no breeze. The curtains hang like wet linen on a clothesline, heavy and thick. Her dresser drawers are empty, her closet hangers aren't used.

"Wasn't always so quiet around here," Meda says, and startles me, because I thought she'd fallen asleep.

"It's nice," I lie, and try to shift on my feet without making any noise.

"You got kids?" she asks. She swivels her head toward me like an owl. "I have kids. All grown now. Grandkids, too. They used to come see me, but they don't like the quiet either."

"You have a radio," I say. "Want me to turn it on?"

"No ma'am. I'm listening to the birds."

I move closer to the window and peer over her shoulder. I don't see any birds, and I don't hear any, either.

"You ever notice how the sky turns blue right before the sun comes all the way over the mountain ridge there?" she asks.

I hadn't noticed. I shake my head.

"You watch tomorrow. It turns blue." She sweeps her cloudy eyes back to the window.

I figure the sky is always blue, unless it's nighttime. I don't have time for skygazing. I wake up at dawn for my shift at the hospital, and I spend evenings doing home visits as a second job. I'm lucky if I get a chance to stare at the TV.

"Where are your clothes?" I ask, searching the empty closet one more time for laundry.

"Right here," says Meda. She points to her dress.

"Don't you have any others?"

"What for?"

"To wear while you're washing something else?"

I've never had to explain this to a grown woman before.

Meda shrugs. "I don't get dirty."

I try looking for dishes, instead. There are none. No messy ones in the sink, no clean ones in the cupboards. "Have you just moved in?" I call from the kitchen.

"Been here nearly five years." Meda's voice is close behind me, and I turn to find her standing in the doorway. "Ever since Amos died. My husband."

I watch her walk to the refrigerator, expecting her to shuffle like the aged woman she is, but her step is light and graceful in her soft sandals. "Did you used to dance?"

She pauses to look at me over her shoulder, her dark eyebrows quirked. "Used to?"

"Like in college or something?"

"What a funny question," she says. She opens her refrigerator door.

Inside, there are more apples than I've seen in my life, piled on every shelf and stuffed into the little compartment drawers at the bottom. Only apples. Yellow or red, or a blend of both, most with a chunk of stem and a couple leaves still attached.

She taps her chin, regarding her stockpile, then she chooses one and offers it to me. "I dance every day, child."

I take the apple, staring past her shoulder at the crammed refrigerator.

She plucks out a fruit for herself and closes the door. "But you're not the kind to understand, I think. You're one of the busy ones."

"What do you mean?"

"Looking to wash my clothes or fix me dinner, eyes roving for whatever chore you can do next."

"Your son is paying me to look after you for two hours. It's only fair I earn the money." I tug at my apple stem, scowling at the thing because it won't pull loose.

Meda puts her soft hand on my fingers. "You can't pull it, child, you have to twist. And try this, while you twist it, say the alphabet."

"What?"

"The alphabet. Whatever letter you stop on when the stem comes off is the letter of the first name of the man you'll marry."

I laugh. "I'll just eat it with the stem on." I take a big, juicy bite.

Meda smiles. She twists her apple stem and only gets as far as "A" before it pops right out. "A. Always A," she says. She carries her apple into her bedroom and settles, ballerina-like, into her rocking chair. "He was a good man, Amos." She nods to herself, her eyes glittering amber in the low evening light.

"You must miss him." I sit on the edge of her bed and take another bite of apple.

"Yes." She sighs. "I didn't expect him to go so soon."

I nod, because I don't know what to say. Grief has always settled strange and uncomfortable onto my shoulders. Scratchy. Like a tweed scarf. I shift, trying to dislodge the feeling.

"Have you lost someone?" Meda asks.

"My mother. When I was seven. She had cancer."

I stand up. "Look, do you have a vacuum cleaner or something?"

Meda looks at me over the back of her chair. "Vacuum cleaner? Do you know how loud those things are?" She shudders. "Why don't you just sit and listen to the birds with me?"

"I don't think that's what your son had in mind when he—"

"Yes it is," she says. "He doesn't come any more, doesn't bring my grandchildren to me. He hired you to fill in the hole where his guilty conscious was leaking."

I wince, because it's been a while since I talked to my father. I sit back down on her bed and listen for birds.

§

While I unlock the front door to my house, the phone is ringing. I toss my keys onto the table and pick up the receiver. "Hello?"

"Hey, it's Kristin."

"Oh, hey. What's up?"

"I just had an emergency come up, could you take my shift tonight?"

I look at my watch. 8:00. "I just got home."

"I know, I'm really sorry. Cammy's already on, and Georgia's out of town. I wouldn't ask, but it's really important."

I rub my eyes.

"I'll take your shift in the morning. If I'm back in

time. I'll make it up to you."

"All right," I say, and shake my head. That's two shifts Kristin owes me, and she's only been working at the hospital for two weeks. "In the morning," I warn her.

I hang up, and change back into my scrubs.

§

Kristin isn't back in the morning. We have two gunshot wounds in ER and a bus rollover by noon. I'm about to take a blood sample of a patient in room three when my supervisor taps me on the arm. "Wrong room. Blood sample's in room two. Have you slept?"

"Got two more hours, then I will."

"Take a break," she says. "I'll draw the sample."

My grumbling stomach leads me down to the cafeteria. I study a fat slice of cherry cheesecake. I sense someone behind me, and twist to find a thirty-something man in blue scrubs and booties holding a fork. He's eyeing the same piece of cake.

"Last piece," he says. "Want to share?" His smile crinkles up the corners of his blue eyes.

"Ah…no. Thanks." I self-consciously smooth my hands over my cheesecake-induced hips.

His eyes follow my hands and his mouth opens to say something else, but I duck away and head for the salad bar.

§

I wobble to Meda Lillin's door, more tired than I ought to be. I've been without sleep plenty of times. I reach up to knock but the door opens and she's standing there, smiling. Then her smile fades.

"You look awful."

"Thanks," I say, and follow her inside.

"You been so busy you can't even sleep?" Meda opens the refrigerator, selects a large yellow apple, and tosses it at me.

My reflexes are slow, but I juggle it around and manage to keep it from hitting the floor. "Double shift at the hospital."

"And you came to see me anyway." She smiles again.

"Your son's—"

"I know," she says, holding up her hand. "It's still nice to have a visitor." She turns to make her way into the bedroom with the picture window. "Maybe one of these days you'll want to come, but not because of the money. When that happens, I'll tell you a secret."

"You can't tell me now?"

"No, you won't believe me. You don't trust me yet."

"I trust you, Meda."

She laughs. It's a soft kind of giggle, like a child's. "You haven't even told me your first name."

"I haven't?"

"No, ma'am." She settles into her rocking chair and stares out the window. "I figure you will when you're good and ready."

I drop onto her bed. "It's Penny."

She leans a brown elbow onto the arm of her brown rocking chair and regards me. "Is that short for something?"

I groan. I've never liked my name. "Short for Penelope," I say. "Why?"

"Makes a difference, most times."

"A difference in what?"

"What it means. Penelope is Greek, but you probably knew that."

I shake my head. "No. What's it mean?"

She smiles. "It means 'girl with a web over her face'."

I don't like my name any better now that I know what it means. I flop onto my back and stare up at her ceiling. "Doesn't matter, anyway. It's just a name."

She makes a sound like 'hmph'. "No such thing as just a name. It's a part of who you are, the blanket that wraps your soul." She leans closer. "Telling someone your name gives them a sort of power over you. They can call on you with it, day or night."

"Yes," I say, growing drowsy on her soft bed. "That's useful for getting someone's attention."

"They can summon you from wherever you are," she says, her voice taking a hard edge. "Ask things of you they got no right to ask. Make you think you want it, too."

I try to respond, but my weary jaw doesn't work. I watch her through slitted eyes while she frowns through the picture window. I can't keep my eyelids from lowering and lowering. I give up and let them fall.

Maybe a few minutes sleep will revive me.

§

I come awake slowly, aware that I'm in a strange bed and that it's dark. I hear children whispering, and they giggle and hush each other. I sit up, startled, and peer around the room.

No one is there.

A cloud shifts to reveal the moon outside. A shadow passes by the glass, gliding silently. Ballerina-like.

"Meda?" I call through the open window.

The shadow moves on.

My watch tells me it's after midnight. My brain reminds me I have to be at the hospital in five hours. I dig for a pen in my purse, leave Meda a note, and hurry home.

§

Around noon the next day I find myself at the dessert display in the cafeteria again. There's no cheesecake, but it's just as well. I'm groggy and faintly cranky from the last few tiring days, and a sugar buzz won't help. I choose a bowl of soup and carry it on a tray toward the cash registers.

Behind me, a man speaks into my ear. "Did you take the last slice of cheesecake?"

I turn to face the thirty-something man from

yesterday. "Soup," I say, and hold up a package of crackers.

He tsks. "Poor substitute. I say we hunt down the perpetrator and make him share. We'll know him by his happy grin and the cherry stain on his tie."

I smile, even though I don't want to. "Violence never solves anything."

"Ah, you speak as one with wisdom," he says. "Let me repay your sage advice by buying your lunch."

"Thanks, but I got it." I receive my change and move toward a table. I eat my soup and crackers in silence.

§

On the way home, I pass by the street that would take me to Meda's house. I'm not scheduled to visit until tomorrow, but I'm a little embarrassed about falling asleep on her bed, and wonder if I ought to explain myself. I circle the block and turn left down her road.

She's checking her mailbox as I pull up. She waves and smiles.

"What a nice surprise," she says, leaning down to talk through my car window. "Want to come in?"

"I just wanted to apologize for dozing off on you last night," I say over the thrum of my idling motor.

"You were tired, poor dear. You should have stayed until morning, we could have watched the sky turn blue."

"I had to get a shower and stuff. But thanks."

She nods. Then she rests her forearm at the top of the door. "I didn't really mean what I said last night about Amos. About knowing my name and talking me into things." Her dark eyes lower. It's the first time she hasn't looked me in the eye.

"I didn't realize you were talking about Amos," I say.

"I did give up a lot to be with him," she says. "And now he's gone and I can never go back. It's hard, sometimes."

I watch her for a few minutes, trying to think of something useful to say. "I have a little time, if you'd like me to stay a while."

She smiles. "Come in and get your apple."

I turn off the motor, grab my purse, and follow her inside. She tosses me an apple the minute I cross the threshold. A red apple, with a tiny smudge of yellow near the stem. "Thanks," I say.

She twists off her stem and holds it up. "Always A."

I consider twisting mine, just for curiosity's sake. I leave it on. "When I woke up last night, I thought I saw you outside the window. I called your name."

She nods. "I heard you. I was hoping you'd follow me."

"Why? What were you doing?"

She lifts her arms, holding her apple, and gracefully pirouettes. "Dancing." Then she steps toward me, takes my hand, and leads me down the hall toward the back door. "Let me show you something."

For some reason, I'm hesitant. "Where are we

going?"

She presses a fist to her hip. "Why, you came to see me, and not because of the money. I can tell you a secret now."

"What kind of secret?" I get the eerie feeling she is going to show me where she buried Amos's body in the back yard.

"Not all news is bad news, Penelope Wilson. Come see something that will make you smile."

I don't know what I'm afraid of. Too embarrassed to admit it, I let her lead me outside.

Her yard is a gentle slope that leads down to a circular clearing of low grass. Pine and laurel trees, just sparse enough to allow bright sunlight, surround the clearing. In the distance, a ridge of rounded mountains is a dramatic backdrop. "It's beautiful," I say.

"Yes," she says, still leading me. "You should see it in the moonlight."

She guides me downward toward the clearing, but stops at the outer edge. A pine branch tickles at my hair. "Walk softly now," she says. "Out into the clearing."

"Alone?" I watch her over my shoulder, but I walk softly.

"Hold out your apple, it's their favorite. And speak quietly, their ears are very sensitive."

"Who's favorite?" I ask. "Whose ears?"

I stare at her from the center of the circle, holding out my apple, and feeling like an idiot.

She looks around through the trees. She murmurs something. She looks back at me with a frown. "They don't much come out in daylight. Try closing your eyes."

I have a few seconds worth of willingness to feel stupid, so I close my eyes. I count. When I reach ten, I'm going to go home.

But I don't get to ten. Around five, I hear soft rustlings like feathers.

Something settles onto my fingers, landing light as a butterfly.

I peep open one eye.

A tiny set of cornflower blue eyes is staring back at me.

Both of my eyes open to find a girl, no taller than the apple in my hand.

Her hair floats, white and ghostlike, in a wisp of a breeze. Her dress, the color of her eyes, haunts around her little form like it's made of whispers.

I gasp. I look to Meda, about to call to her, but she presses her finger to her mouth.

"Sssh."

I watch as the girl takes a miniscule bite of apple.

She giggles, and darts into the air on fluttery wings I hadn't noticed before. She swoops once.

Then another girl appears, this one with dark hair and skin of bronze. She drifts down to land on the apple and delicately sits.

Another comes, and another, and then groups of them, all drifting on wings in a multi-colored array. Each lands somewhere on my outstretched arm, or my shoulder, or on top of my head.

I stand very still; too distracted by the wonder of it

all to remember it can't possibly be real.

I lose count of my little visitors. When there is no more room to alight onto my arm, they simply hover near it. I watch them.

They watch me watching them.

"Hello," I whisper.

"Hello!" come their voices in melodic unison. Then they squeal with laughter, burst into the air in a shimmer of wings and quivering skirts, and flutter away.

I lower my arm and let the apple drop to the ground. I turn my eyes to Meda, and stare. "Am I hallucinating? Or did I just get mobbed by a group of…." I can't bring myself to say it.

"Fairies," she says.

"That was amazing."

"Yes," she says.

"I can't tell anyone, or they'll think I'm crazy."

"Yes," she says again.

I smile. "This is your secret, isn't it? Because if there's something else, I'm not sure I can handle it."

She laughs. "It is my secret." She turns to make her way back up the slope, her elderly body light on its toes. Delicate. I watch her while I follow.

"Meda?"

"Hm?"

"How do you know them?"

"The fairies?" She holds open the back door for me to walk through. "They visit me. We dance together."

"But, why? Why do they come?"

She tips her head, studying me.

"You're one of them, somehow, aren't you?" I ask.

She's still for a time. Quiet. Then she shakes her head. "No, not one of them. I can't ever really go back." She walks through the hall on soundless feet and waits for me at the front door.

I'm halfway down the walk before I pause. I turn. She's on the porch step, her arms crossed.

"Was it worth it?" I ask. "Giving up so much?"

She releases a long, silent breath. "It's hard now, without him. But I'm not the first to give so much, and I hope I'm not the last." She smiles. "It was worth it. Love always is."

§

I'm in the cafeteria at the hospital, drowsy again because I couldn't sleep. I was thoughtful, preoccupied with memories of my visitors in Meda's clearing. I wonder, even now, standing near the salad bar, if I really saw what I think I did.

I have an apple in my hand. I'm looking at the stem.

I glance around myself, but no one is watching, they're busy talking and choosing their own lunch. So I pinch my fingers around the apple stem and twist. A. B. C. D. E. F. G. H.

Out pops the stem. H.

I hear a voice behind me. A voice I'm beginning to recognize. "We meet again."

I turn to face the blue-eyed, thirty-something

man wearing scrubs and matching booties. "Yes," I say. "Again."

"An apple today," he says, pointing to the fruit in my hand. "That shatters the old adage about keeping the doctor away. Because here I am."

I smile and nod, but I'm considering waving the fruit at him to see if it might work, after all.

"So, um," he says into the awkward silence. "I'm Hemingway Flanders. I lurk around the second floor."

"Oh, Dr. Flanders, sure." I've heard of him. Internal medicine. "Your first name is Hemingway?"

He winces. "My mother's a fan. I consider myself lucky she doesn't read Poe."

I laugh, and he smiles in that way that crinkles up his eyes. I take a deep breath. "I see there's a slice of cherry cheesecake in the display."

He looks over his shoulder, then back at me. "Last piece."

I nod. I drop the apple stem into the pocket of my scrubs and then jut out my hand for a shake. "I'm Penny Wilson," I say. "Want to share?"

LATE

Railcars squealing

shaking the road

rocking

wheels like thunder

a storm passing

forcing me to wait

while my hopes

like a hobo

travel the tracks

and disappear into

the rain

MIRROR, MIRROR ON THE WALL

Elizabeth was frightened of her own face.

Each time she peered cautiously at this mirror—her breath held, her heart secretly hoping for a new reflection on a new day—she startled. Shadows deepened the vicious line of her mouth. Her brows creased with terrifying anger. And her eyes. When she could bring herself to examine her eyes, they churned with the rage of a black sea gnawing at its shoreline.

Most days, she couldn't look that long.

She had other mirrors, and they were kinder. A tall one helped her see herself from the braid of her auburn hair against her forehead, to the floor-brushing lace of her gown. Another cast a light that softened her features, made them younger. Yet another reflection smiled endlessly, even when she scowled at it, and her mood brightened whenever she played its games.

She was, in fact, surrounded by mirrors, and each one rendered her just a little differently than every other.

"One day," she said to her smiling mirror, "I am going to see the real me."

"You are very special," said the mirror.

Elizabeth nodded, but turned away from her reflection to stare out the window into the courtyard below. She watched butter-yellow lady slippers bump against arching stalks of lavender; she saw a chubby bumblebee inspecting a primrose. All of spring was bright with expectation. But Elizabeth felt it as a barb, catching on the ragged edge of her soul.

For one mirror, the one she hated, perched at the foot of the bed and taunted her. Tempted her to look. "I am the real you," it whispered. "See me and believe."

"I will not!" Elizabeth shouted suddenly. Every mirror in the room drew a breath. Even her smiling reflection dimmed in alarm. Elizabeth ignored them all and turned her bitterness to that vicious reflection on her velvet bedcover.

"I will not look at you," she snarled. "I will not believe you." She lifted the mirror above her head, carried it to the open window, and reared back to cast it into the courtyard below.

"Mommy!"

She spun away from the window. "What is it? Who is there?"

"Mommy! Let me go!" A disembodied voice emanated from her hated mirror, and in surprise, she looked into its glass.

Shadows deepened the vicious line of her mouth. Her brows creased with terrifying anger.

"Go away!" she shouted at the mirror. She threw it to the floor.

It thudded louder than she'd expected it to land. It cried out.

"Elizabeth! My God," said another voice.

Childlike wails filled the room and pained her ears. Footsteps throbbed across the stone floor. Voices babbled over voices, and she stood among them, confused.

But then, the hated mirror did as she told. It went away.

"Ssh," said a voice above the din of desolate crying. "There, there. Let's let Mommy have her rest." A door closed.

After a moment, she heard another voice. "Shall I brush your hair? It always makes you feel better."

Elizabeth turned to her smiling reflection and released a long breath. "Yes. Thank you."

She walked to her vanity, sat in her chair, and adjusted her skirts comfortably. In moments, the scrape of a brush eased over her scalp, and she closed her eyes.

"I like you best," she said. "I hope you're the real one."

"You are very special," said the mirror.

EMET FOLEY'S BABY

Rhea May felt the shudder of each thunderclap in the rocks beneath her bare feet. She was climbing fast down the trail, struggling with her baby sister in her arms, while rain stung like a willow branch against her face and soaked her trousers.

She paused to squint. She knew these Arkansas mountains better than anyone in Searcy County. Even her daddy had said so once or twice. She'd spent all her thirteen years memorizing the ravines and crags, knowing the old black oak and jack pine trees like friends. But the trail didn't seem so friendly tonight, with the storm slapping her back and the trail gone slick with mud.

A flash of lightning showed her the hump of stone near the ridge where MizElvina's cabin squatted, waiting. Most folks avoided MizElvina the way they avoided the gulch that veered off near Crooked Creek; they both looked just dangerous enough not to take any chances. And with MizElvina's way of knowing things other folks believed ought to be left to the Good Lord to know, Rhea May could see why the old Black woman didn't get much company.

But Rhea May wasn't afraid of the gulch, or of MizElvina. Only one thing in the world Rhea May feared, and she was praying hard she wouldn't have to face him when she got back home.

When Rhea May reached the cabin, MizElvina was already in the doorway, holding her apron over her head against the rain. Her gray, wiry hair was beaded with water. "Rhea May Foley, you picked a fine night to visit."

"Tell my mama. Ain't my choice."

"You're wetter than the split peas I got soaking for soup. You and that youngin you got, there." MizElvina turned toward her stone fireplace, shaking water from her apron.

Rhea May ducked through the door and followed the shuffling woman toward the heat. "I got to get back before Daddy," said Rhea May. "Took too long already, back of my neck's telling me he's about home."

"What's your daddy doing tromping around in the storm?" MizElvina took the baby and peeked at her pale skin under the drenched blanket.

Rhea May rubbed the cramps from her wrists. "I turned out Old Scout, Daddy's best hunter. Said he run off."

MizElvina chuckled. "Clever." She turned her back, and Rhea May watched the woman's fleshy arms while she unwrapped and then fastened the baby into a dry quilt.

"She ain't made a sound since she took a breath," said Rhea May. "She going to be all right?"

"Yes," MizElvina said over her shoulder. "Your mama still quiet, too?"

"Yes'm."

"How much did you give her?"

"Two pinches," said Rhea May. "Into a cup of milk, like you told me."

"When?"

"Right when I seen the baby's head coming."

MizElvina nodded. She set the baby into a wicker basket, and then reached around the kitchen door for a jar of dried lima beans. "She ought to start rousing about the time you get back. Take this jar, wrap it with a fresh cloth, and put it right into the box, you hear?"

"Yes'm." Rhea May hugged the jar to her chest. Just the right weight. Felt like she was carrying her sister again.

Rhea May didn't have time to pause, but she did anyway. "You won't tell her what I done, right? When she's older?"

MizElvina just stared with calm eyes.

Rhea May glanced at the baby in the basket. To her surprise, she felt a bristle of tears behind her eyes. She made for the door before MizElvina could see, plunging back into the storm.

Just as she was rounding a boulder that marked the corner of their property, she heard a shout.

"Rhea May!" Her father's voice. He was coming up behind her.

She knew he had Old Scout by the collar, because she could hear the dog panting and whimpering, drawing closer. For a second, her heart went cold. Then lightning sputtered, and she hunched her shoulders against the bean jar and sprinted through the craggy front door.

She ran to the room where she'd left Mama, who was still wide-eyed and staring at the ceiling. She pulled a wooden box from beneath the bed and set the bean jar inside it, hastily tucking an old rag around it. Then she worked the lid down onto the wood with shaking hands. She set the box onto the bed. "It's going to be all right," she whispered, and kissed Mama's warm forehead.

Mama blinked. She made a quiet sound. Rhea May covered her twitching legs with a blanket.

"Rhea May?" Pristine, the five-year-old, poked her golden head into the room. "Can we come down now?"

The twins came in, their faces somber and their blonde braids dangling against matching, rumpled flannel. "We been waiting real quiet," said Eileen.

"Where's the baby?" asked Shyleen.

Rhea May pointed to the tiny coffin on the bed. The three girls gasped.

"Rhea May! Girl!" Daddy stomped toward the bedroom doorway, his boots squashing watery prints onto the floor. "I been calling you. You ignoring me?"

He leaned a wide shoulder against the frame.

"No, sir," she said, her throat tight.

He narrowed his eyes, then turned them to Mama, who was quietly moaning. "That baby come yet?"

"Yes, sir."

"Well?"

Rhea May swallowed hard. The last time she'd lied to Daddy, she was six years old, and she'd eaten the last plate of apple cobbler. She'd never forgotten that beating. She tried real hard to form words around the lie she knew she had to tell tonight. She looked right into Daddy's brown eyes.

"Well?" asked Daddy.

"The baby's in the box," said Pristine, tugging on Daddy's pant leg. Eileen and Shyleen sat on the bed next to Mama and touched her hand.

"It's dead?" he asked.

Rhea May lifted the small box. "I came looking to tell you. I took care of it."

Daddy reached a hand like he was going to peek inside. "What was it?"

"A girl," said Rhea May.

Daddy's hand recoiled. Then he looked again at Mama. "Figures." He ran his hand through his wet hair, eyes lingering on her. "She don't look right. She sick?"

"Just real tired."

Daddy looked from Pristine to Eileen, to Shyleen, and finally to Rhea May. "I told your Mama if she gave me another girl I was going to smother it dead. Least she saved me the trouble." He shook his head and turned for the door. "You girls get yourself to bed, it's late."

"Can I stay with Mama?" asked Rhea May.

"Suit yourself," said Daddy. He left to sleep by the fire.

Rhea May had thought facing Daddy was going to be the hardest part of her lie, but soon Mama started crying and asking for the baby, and Rhea May had to hold her hand and tell her the baby was gone.

"Gone," Mama wailed. "My little baby gone."

"Yes'm," said Rhea May, wanting to cry, too. "But she's in a better place now. I promise."

Mama's tears turned quiet, and finally, about the time the gray dawn lit the sill of the knotty window frame, Mama was asleep.

But not Rhea May. She crept out of bed, put on one of Daddy's clean shirts, and carried out the casket.

Daddy was awake, too. He met Rhea May at the front door. "Your mama, she all right?"

Rhea May stared at Daddy, frozen.

"She cried a lot, I could hear it."

Rhea May managed a nod.

Finally, Daddy opened the door. He plucked a shovel from the stoop. He didn't say another word, all the way down the mountain and across the meadow still slick from last night's storm. When they got to the plot of land all the neighbors used as a cemetery, he started to dig.

Together, in silence, Rhea May and Daddy buried a jar of dried lima beans.

WARRIOR

While the sound of slamming doors

rings your ears

stings your soul

while the sound of screaming silence

thumps your heart

lumps your throat

others look but only see

an average Joe

or Emily

but those of us

who've walked that darkness

know you

warrior

friend

THE TIME SCAR
PART ONE

"This is not our war. This is not our fight."

Del Tomas watched as a farmer pressed his dirtied hands to his brow. "It's dangerous to go," said the farmer. "But it's more dangerous to stay. My family will join." The man's shoulders sagged.

In the cellar, a single candle burned in the center of a rugged table. Del counted seventeen faces hovering in the light. Seventeen simple men with families to protect.

No one knew why it had come to this. For a few weeks now, rumors had been whispered about border tension between Tirchess Territory, to the east, and Gellwydra Territory, here in the south, but no one was prepared for the war that was suddenly upon them all.

It had erupted quickly. Too quickly for the capital city of Elonra to send warnings out to even the larger towns with telephone lines. Too quickly for the telegraph. Here in the farming village of Cooperborough, their only saving grace was the traveling bag man from neighboring Lintswich who'd stopped in the night for a rest in Del's father's barn and brought the news of violence with him.

A war between dragons, with ancient roots and powerful magics, and helpless humans trapped between them.

So, farmers of Coopersborough gathered in Del's father's cellar, crammed against walls and wedged together in darkness, trying to figure out what to do.

Del was squeezed so tightly against his younger cousin, Aveen, he could feel her breathing.

He tried not to breathe. The air tasted like mud. He tried not to move, because it only burrowed Aveen's elbow harder into his upper thigh. But there was something else in the air of that room that made it hard to move and to breathe. Del tasted that, too, and every time he pulled it through his nostrils, it took a little more of him.

Fear. So raw it turned his pulse to hammer strikes.

It was his father's turn to speak. The last of the seventeen. "It was war that brought my grandfather to this land," Del's father said, patting a soiled handkerchief to his upper lip. "I'm sure he was as torn to leave his homeland as I am, but he followed his convictions." His voice broke.

Del's mother gripped his father's shoulder, wrinkling the knuckles of her pale hand.

"Then it's settled," said Greg Donnis, the youngest

father at the table. "If any other families change their mind before dawn, we'll bring them. But we must leave at dawn. The Tirchess dragons will be upon us if we don't."

"Yes. Four hours," said Del's father. He reached up to hold the hand on his shoulder. "My family is packed and ready. If anyone needs help—"

"If you could spare Del," said Uncle Randall, who raised a hand. "I'll need a hand hitching the trailer to our lorry."

A sudden clap of thunder sent a ripple of panic through the cellar.

"Not rain," someone cried. "Not now."

Bodies shivered and began to funnel up the stairs.

Del was swept into the crush. His feet kicked against the bottom step, and he stumbled up.

Aveen clutched at his arm. He managed to tug her onto his hip. Just as he was about to make the final step up into the building, he was stopped. The mass of bodies that had dragged him up had become a wall of silence. "Move on," he said, and elbowed someone's spine.

"Del? Is it dawn already?" Aveen pointed through the ironwork of a tiny window.

In the distance, at the curve of the hill near the village center, Del saw a glowing arc of orange light.

"That's not sunrise," said Del.

Just then, the town's warning bells began screeching.

The wall ahead of him broke into flailing arms and running legs. He cut through the panic to lunge out into the night. He fought the urge to run, and waited instead for his parents as Aveen clung to his side with strength he didn't think a six-year-old could have.

"Where's Daddy?" she asked.

Del could see her wide, blue eyes even in the dark. "He'll be here," said Del.

A hand gripped his elbow. His father. "They've cut off the south exit," he said. "Take Aveen to the north road. I'll help Randy with his trailer."

"But—"

"Tell everyone you see to go with you. I'll do the same. I'll meet you there as soon as I can."

Del would have argued, but his father was gone.

"Where's Daddy?" Aveen asked again.

Del glanced around for Uncle Randall, but his eyes caught on the rage of red fire in the distance. Two massive, dragon-shaped shadows swerved in and out of the light, spitting sparks into a grove of trees.

"I want Daddy." Aveen tried to wrestle out of his arms.

"I know. My dad is helping him hitch the trailer. They'll meet us at the north road. Come on, we've got to go." He switched her to his other hip. He wanted to stay with his father and mother, too, but he obeyed, and loped as fast as he could toward the high end of the village.

He passed Greg Donnis, who was slinging a saddlebag over his horse. His two boys straddled the mare. His wife was crying silently.

"My father said to meet at the north road," Del

said.

"Right behind you," Greg said.

Then came a deafening screech, like the swing of a giant, rusty door.

Aveen slapped her hands over her ears.

Del felt the earth rumble right through his boots.

"About time," said Greg. He glanced up at three more descending dragon shapes, and then tugged his horse northward.

Three Gellwydra dragons, defenders from this side of the border, glided in against gray cloud cover, and then swooped low, right over Del's head. They came so close he could have reached up to touch a scaled belly.

He felt the slam of air as wings beat hard. He even smelled them. Like moss in the oak trees after a heavy rain.

"They want Daddy!" Aveen tried to wrench from his hands.

"No, they're going to help us." He grabbed at her arms, but she was flailing. "Stop it, Aveen! We have to meet him on the road!"

She went limp, and Del couldn't adjust quickly enough. She slid down his leg like she was coated in bacon grease and flopped to the ground. Then she jumped to her feet and started running. South.

Del chased after her. "You're going the wrong way!"

She was quick, but Del's legs were long. He reached her, just about to grab the collar of her dress, when a shower of sparks blinded him. His hair sizzled. His bare arms stung.

Dragon cries turned to caterwauling. A column of fire hit the path just feet away. The village erupted with screams, and people scattered, dragging children, diving behind steam tractors or vehicles, running to hide.

Del coughed on smoke. His eyes watered. He stumbled forward, his shoulder bumping people running the other way. "Aveen! Come back!"

"Del!"

A familiar voice. He turned to find his father, arms open, with soot smeared across his forehead.

Del knew he was too old to cry, but he almost did, anyway. "I can't find Aveen. She ran."

"She what?" His father's arms dropped.

"She ran. I tried to catch her, but I can't see in all this smoke."

"Come on. We can't let her get to her house." Del's father grabbed his arm and pushed him ahead.

"Why? Where's Uncle Randall?"

He didn't answer.

"Father?"

His father shook his head. "The Gellwydra dragons tried to pull the Tirchess pair further south, but they were determined. They kept circling back. They kept heading straight for Randy's farm."

"Why?"

Del looked over his shoulder to see his father staring south, his eyes wide. He followed his father's gaze.

Uncle Randall's house was an inferno, blazing so hot that even from several yards away, Del had to shield his face.

He heard his father moan. "Aveen."

"Here," came a faint voice.

Del's eyes were drawn toward the open lot in front of the farmhouse path. There, stretched out and panting, lay a dragon so pale that the flaming house turned it orange. It wore a saddle with white stitching. A Gellwydra dragon.

And then, several yards away, movement caught Del's eye. At first, he thought it was just a puff of smoke from the burning house, but it paused. In that moment, through haze, he locked eyes with a shadow. Flames sputtered, lighting the darkness, and Del thought he recognized Uncle Randy, hunched and watching. But this man was old, with wrinkled skin and white eyebrows, as though Uncle Randy had aged thirty years.

Then sparks of flame stung Del's eyes. He shielded them with his hands, but when he squinted at the place where he'd seen the man, no one was there.

"Del," said his father, tugging him aside, toward the felled dragon. They both crept toward her.

The dragon's massive head lolled toward them, thick lashes closing against dull eyes. That's when Del caught a new scent. Something bitter, and even stronger than the creature's dank scales. Del's foot slipped. He looked down to find his boot in a puddle of wetness.

"Blood," whispered his father. "She's dying."

The dragon wheezed through clenched teeth. "Take the child." She relaxed her wing, and it fell aside to reveal Aveen, crying and holding a gold disk in her little hands.

"Don't go, Daddy!" she wailed at the disk. "Don't go!"

"Aveen." Del's father's voice came in a rush of breath, and he lunged forward.

"Moors," said the dragon. "The child has the map. Go."

"We can't reach the moors," said Del's father, lifting Aveen into his arm.

Aveen clutched him, sobbing into his shoulder. The disk dropped from her fingers and dangled on a silver chain.

"We'll have to go east," said Del's father.

"Fault." The dragon's head sagged, and a froth of blood oozed from the corner of her mouth. Then she was very still.

"No, old girl. It wasn't your fault." Del's father patted the dead dragon's head.

Aveen was still crying, and in the blaze of her burning home, her blue eyes were violet. She stared at Del over his father's shoulder.

A gout of flame erupted ahead of them. Four dragons grappled in the sky, two were diving toward the village, and two were swooping around to blast fire in their path.

"Let's go!" shouted Del's father.

They ran past columns of smoke that were once trees or fences, past villagers staring out of locked windows.

His father's breathing turned ragged. He slowed.

Del silently tugged Aveen over to himself and urged his father on.

§

They reached the north road out of town. Families grouped along the curbs. There were three horses and two sedans, and one truck full of straw and boxes. Most people carried heavy packs on their backs, even some of the children. Some were coughing. All were staring into the sky.

Del's mother was among them. She saw the three coming and clutched her hands to her stomach. "Oh! Oh, James," she said to Del's father as she hurried toward them, then looked past them toward the village. "Where's Randall?"

Del couldn't see his father's face, but he could see his mother's. Tears welled, and she pressed wrinkled hands to her cheeks. "Oh, my dear brother."

"Daddy..." Aveen wailed in Del's arms.

For a split second, Del thought about telling them what he saw back at the house, about Uncle Randall appearing, old and hunched, but... what *did* he see, exactly? The old man had disappeared a moment later. Del was too confused about it to know how to explain it.

"We'll have to go east," said Del's father.

"No!" cried Aveen. "The moors! The dragon said the moors!"

Greg Donnis stepped forward. "East is nothing but

forest. You aren't suggesting we carve a path through the trees?"

Del's father shook his head. "We can follow the treeline. Northeast."

Someone screamed. Shouts broke out.

"James," said Del's mother. "They're coming."

Del spun.

Two pairs of dark wings pulled in against dark bodies and dove straight for the road. Gellwydra dragons threw themselves into those bodies and knocked them off course.

"Are they following us? Hunting us?" asked Del's mother.

"That doesn't make sense." Greg Donnis turned to grab the reins of his horse and led his boys north. "But if we go east," he continued, "We're offroading for miles. If we go north, we've got a straight road toward the moors near Shersborough. Then, onto Elonra. If the Tirchess dragons *are* following us, they won't dare go as far as the capital."

With a screech of pain, a Gellwydra dragon dropped from sky and landed hard. It quaked the ground as though to split it open. The rumble drowned any other sound, and if Del's father was arguing, Del couldn't hear it.

Sixteen families surged forward, on horses, in vehicles, and on foot. North, toward the moors.

§

When the road hit a dead-end at a field of waist-high cornstalks, the group fractured into individuals driving and pushing their way toward the other side. As Del walked, he heard people beside him and behind him; men and women were shouting directions and warnings out of vehicle windows and over horse heads.

When Del paused to look over his shoulder toward the battling dragons, his mother gripped his back and pushed him on.

"Forward, Del," she said. "Keep looking forward."

Aveen was ahead, running alongside Greg Donnis and his horse.

"Where's Father?" Del asked.

"Right behind you. Don't worry," said his mother.

Del's father then pushed past him. "We're almost to the paved road again. Hurry, Son."

Del hurried past the cars in the middle of the caravan. He caught up to Aveen, who had paused to wait. Her eyes were solemn and still damp with tears.

"It's going to be all right," Del said.

She just turned and pushed onward.

Behind him, a dragon cry sounded so close he tensed, waiting for a swoop and the clutch of dragon claws.

His mother's hand tightened on his back.

He kept moving.

Finally, he broke through the cornfield into open space. Just ahead, families were regrouping. Children were lifted into arms. People traded seats in jalopies, and someone climbed out of a truck bed to walk.

"We'll barely get across town before dawn," said Del. "We'll be caravanning in broad daylight."

"They won't follow us that far, will they, James?" asked Del's mother, turning her face to them, her skin as pale as a patch of moonflowers.

"They shouldn't have cared to follow us *this* far, but they're still back there," said Del's father. "Once we get through the next town, we'll have to watch for places on the road we could duck into."

"I don't understand why Tirchess sent their dragons all the way to us." Del's mother reached for Aveen and picked her up to carry her. "We have nothing to do with their border wars."

"They want Daddy," said Aveen, and hugged her arms around her aunt's neck.

"I don't know, Margaret. I don't understand it either," Del's father said, behind them. "The Gellwydra fighters are holding them off, but they're—look out!" He dove forward, knocking Del's mother and Aveen to the ground, flattening himself over them.

"Father!" Del shouted, frozen and staring as a spout of fire spat down from the sky and blasted at his father's back.

A roar sounded, and Del felt a descending rush of weight like a plummeting boulder.

He dove, then, too, and covered his head with his arms.

Something thudded beside him.

He peered up to see a bright green dragon crouched over his family, shielding them, taking the full blast of the flames. Then it sprang, mouth open and claws thrust upward, swallowing the fire as it propelled toward the attacker.

Del crawled to his father, who lay motionless, his overalls charred and smoking. "Father?"

"Del!" his mother cried, trying to shift beneath heavy weight. "He's not moving!"

"Uncle James, let me up!" Aveen shrieked.

Del could see her blonde braids coiled under his father's shoulder.

His father groaned.

Del lunged forward to grasp his shoulder. "Father, we have to keep moving."

"Can't," he said, his face pressed into the ground. "Go. You go."

"No!" Del's mother rose up from beneath him as a geyser of stubborn strength. She arched her back, climbing to her hands and knees hoisting him from the ground.

Aveen scrambled out, the frayed edge of her skirt smoldering.

Del's mother continued lifting until she stood with his father's arms over her shoulders and his feet dragging the ground. "Go, James Thomas! Walk!" And she loped forward, dragging him against her back.

Del found his feet, too, and pulled Aveen into the forest trees.

"That dragon," said his mother, her voice strained as she struggled with her cargo. "It protected us."

"Yes," said Del.

"Is it alive?"

Del looked back.

Through the branches and across the sky, a speck of dawn struggled to shine on the horizon. Fingers of gray light pulled back the darkness.

"I don't see anything," he said. He realized he didn't hear anything, either.

"Come on, Del," said Aveen. She tugged at his arm.

His mother was already several steps ahead, approaching Greg Donnis and his horse. The Donnis boys slid from the horse's back to make room for Del's father. Other stragglers gathered around to help Del's mother.

One of his father's shoes had caught on the edge of the path and had been pulled loose. Del scooped it up and hurried behind his mother. "How is he?" he asked.

"He's breathing, but not moving. Catch up to the others and don't wait for us. Hurry."

"I can't leave you." Del shoved his father's shoe into a saddlebag.

"Yes, you can, Del. Aveen must be kept safe, no matter the cost."

"What do you mean?" He looked down at his little cousin, who was crying again.

Del's mother strained, with the help of the others, to lift Del's unconscious father onto the back of the horse.

"What do you mean?" Del asked again.

"Your uncle hasn't always been just a farmer," said Del's mother. "I don't know everything about my brother, but if those Tirchess dragons really are following us…" She gave one last push to balance Del's father across the horse's spine. Then she turned back to Del, out of breath. "Randy told me once that Aveen is very important. I believe him, Del. She's been a little different, and a lot like him, all these years."

Del still didn't understand what his mother was trying to say, but he saw the desperation in her eyes. Her fear. Now was a good time for obedience, not argument. He kissed his mother's warm, damp cheek. "I'll send back help." Then he plunged onward, despite feeling he was leaving the most important parts of himself behind.

Eventually, he and Aveen reached Eastshire. The town was familiar enough to him, he'd spent countless summer days sneaking into movie theaters and chasing friends through corner stores here. But now, the town had gone silent, full of abandoned cars and ransacked storefronts. Eastshire had always been unkempt and a little dodgy, but he had no idea the place had gotten so bad. Had the dragon war driven them out?

They walked along the disheveled main street. More than once his feet caught, and he nearly fell onto Aveen. When his arms gave out, he had to switch her piggyback. Even then, he grew tired from her weight, but he continued on, spooked by the eerie silence. He could hear his own feet, clumsy along the road, but nothing else.

"I think we're going the wrong way," he said. "It's too quiet."

"It's that way." Aveen pointed over his shoulder.

Ahead and to the right, he saw a ramshackle train tunnel.

Del paused. Shadows dipped in and out of the passageway, and fat, green vines swayed across the opening. "I don't think the others went that way," he said.

"It's that way," Aveen said. He felt her cheek rest against his left shoulder blade.

Still, he hesitated. Then he heard voices. Or, what might have been voices, very distant and muffled. He carried Aveen closer to the tunnel and leaned toward the vine-covered entrance to listen.

"Do you hear that?" Del asked. "I can't tell if it's people or the wind."

"It's whispers," said Aveen. Then she shifted suddenly and squirmed, trying to drop off his back. "That dragon is coming!"

He tried to keep a grip on his cousin, but couldn't. "The green one?" he asked.

"No!" She jumped up so quickly she smacked into the back of his legs. Then she ran past him and into the shadowy tunnel.

"Aveen, wait!" He dove after her.

Heat exploded behind him. He was thrown to the ground, and for the second time, he covered his head with his arms, and felt his breath stop while he waited for the blind panic to pass.

Aveen tugged at his shirt. "Come on, Del! Hurry!"

He blinked up at her. Her eyes were wide, her face a red blotch like she'd been in the sun too long. "Come on!" she said again.

He climbed to his feet. Heat clawed at his back, and he turned to see the opening of the tunnel rimmed with flames. Gray smoke rose, obscuring the way they'd just come in.

"I don't think he'll come in," said Aveen, her voice breathy.

As she spoke, Del caught sight of a yellow eye through the haze.

A dragon roar erupted, quivering the ground and blasting the smoke away with a sharp gust. Del looked straight into the bogwater-brown, scaly face of a Tirchess dragon.

Then the smoke billowed over to cover the opening again. Del turned to run, gripping Aveen's hand. "Forward," he said. "Just keep looking forward."

Forward they ran.

§

"I can't walk anymore, Aveen, let's just stop for a second." Del swerved to sit on a thigh-high boulder jutting from the tunnel floor.

He watched Aveen, her eyes intent on the path ahead of them. She waited but rolled her feet up to her toes and down, over and over, eager to keep moving.

Del couldn't figure out where the child's energy was coming from. "Don't you want to sit?"

"I'm not tired. I want to help Daddy."

Del sighed. Uncle Randall was well beyond help,

but he knew arguing with her wouldn't do any good. Let the kid think she was on a mission. At least it kept her from lagging behind.

Right now, Del was the one struggling to keep moving. He'd been up since before dawn and had been running for his life since. This old train tunnel didn't help matters; it was quiet and cool and went on for what seemed like miles ahead of them. "I don't know how we're ever going to find the others now. I don't know where we are."

"They'll find us. But not if we keep sitting here." Aveen trampled over a piece of ruined track and then yanked on his shirt sleeve. "Come on. I hear the whispers telling us to hurry."

"Uh." Del regarded his cousin, looked around himself, and then met Aveen's eyes again. "Whispers?"

"Don't you hear them? You did before."

"No, I heard the wind or something."

"It wasn't the wind." Aveen frowned. "I'm not making it up. Listen."

Del listened. At first, he heard nothing, then he recognized the sound of delicate leaves twisting in faint wind and brushing each other. It was almost a whisper if he turned his head just right. He looked up at the intermittent gaps in the tunnel ceiling; vines and tree branches were visible where bricks had come loose and wooden struts had rotted away.

Then, beneath the whispering of leaves came another sound. Maybe it had been there all along, he just hadn't realized. "Is that water?" He stood. "I hear a waterfall."

"I don't want to swim," Aveen said.

"Aren't you thirsty?" Del's mouth felt like dry leather. He dragged his tongue over his cracked lips. "I wish we'd brought something to carry it in." He moved on, listening for the rush of water. A glance over his shoulder found a scowling Aveen, but he kept walking anyway, looking in the shadowy edges of the tunnel for maintenance doors or cracks in the walls. They would need water, especially if they were going to be out here for a while.

He saw an old wooden door in the wall, so gray and dusty it nearly disappeared into the stone around it.

"Yes, I'm thirsty, but that's the wrong way. We need to follow the tunnel."

"How do you know?" Del tried the iron handle of the door. It was stuck fast. He pushed on the door with his shoulder, then slammed into it with all his weight.

The door burst open, and he stumbled onto a concrete staircase carved into a hill. Surprised, he looked over his shoulder at Aveen. She crossed her arms.

"How do you know the others went down the tunnel?" he asked her.

"They didn't," said Aveen.

Now Del was the one to cross his arms. "But you said--"

"I said I want to help Daddy. We need to go the way the dragon said."

He turned back to the staircase. He eyed the rusted, sharp looking remains of a handrail, and began to carefully follow the upward curve of what was left of the crumbling steps. "Which dragon?" he called.

At the top, he emerged into daylight. Into forest.

Sure enough, just a few feet away, a swollen creek rambled between sparse elm trees and ivy ground cover. He forgot his question and shouted, "There is water!" Del worked to squeeze through the green brush and out into the open.

He felt Aveen tugging at his trouser leg. "We shouldn't be up here."

"We'll just get a drink and then keep going," he said. When he was at the crest of a short hill, he hurried to the creek bank and knelt to cup his hand into the cool water.

"Aveen, you should drink, too." He stood and brushed at the knees of his trousers.

She was already there, standing at the edge of the water and dipping her hand into the crystal depths.

"I'm going to see what feeds it." His feet crunched along the bank as he turned to explore.

"I thought you said we could keep going!"

"We will! But if we're near the others, we could find them and lead them to water."

Aveen frowned.

"I'm worried about my mother and father. Aren't you?" he asked.

Her frown faded. She nodded.

"And the others. Aren't you wondering if they're safe?"

She nodded again.

"So, let's be smart about this, all right? That tunnel has gotten us this far, but we're in the middle of nowhere now. We can't just keep wandering around without a plan."

Her bottom lip began to quiver.

Del tried to head it off by distracting her. "Let's see what feeds the creek." He turned his back so if she did start crying, he wouldn't have to watch.

He plucked along the bank, which was spongy moss and littered with sharp rocks. Twice he slipped, and twice he slashed his fingers when he struggled for grip. Whenever he looked back for Aveen, she was following along with a frown on her face. "Doing all right?" he called once.

"Yes," she said.

Finally, he heard a quiet rumble, like the low groan of a gathering thundercloud. The air around them felt thicker, and so damp he thought if he reached out, he could close his fingers around its wetness. "Hey, I think we're close." He hurried on, and, sure enough, as he crested a small hill, the sight of a narrow and high waterfall broke through parted trees.

"There it is, Aveen, look." He pointed, looking back to find Aveen pushing past him and splashing through the shallow water at the creek's bank.

"Pretty." She stood in front of him with her hands on her hips, staring off at the rush of falling water.

It was a small waterfall, but still fascinating to watch. Cliff stones jutted out at interesting angles and stuck through the water to form a sort of staircase. The water bounced onto one shelf, knocked over to another, and then continued to clatter down the cliff to hit with a splash into the creek that peacefully went on its way.

"Yeah, pretty," said Del.

"Now can we go?" Aveen peered over her shoulder at him.

"Aveen." He stepped toward her to put his hand on her head. "How do you know where that tunnel leads? I'm supposed to keep you safe. I promised."

"The tunnel leads to Daddy. He needs me to go there."

"How do you know that, though?" asked Del.

Aveen reached around her neck and pulled out a chain. On the chain dangled the gold disk Del had seen earlier. He'd forgotten about it. "The pale dragon gave it to me," said Aveen.

Del strained to remember what had been said. Everything was happening too fast at the time, and he'd been startled by the house fire and the ghost of Uncle Randy—or whatever that had been. "Did she say it was a map?" Del asked.

Aveen nodded. "To the moors. To help Daddy."

Maybe Del had been too indulgent in letting her think she was on a mission or something. Letting her pretend in order to keep her moving was one thing, but this.... He shook his head. "Look, I think we—"

"You lied to me."

"No, I didn't," he said. "Just... the fire, and everything. What if your father was...?"

"He wasn't." Aveen lifted her chin and stared at

him, as bold and determined as any grownup had ever looked at him. His mother wasn't wrong when she'd said Aveen had always been a little different. His cousin was showing that now; sure of herself, seeming older than she was, somehow. "Stay here and stare at the water if you want," she said. "I need to find my daddy."

"You can't go off by yourself."

"Watch me." She nudged past him, heading back.

He darted his hand to catch her shoulder. She yanked away from him and broke into a run.

He lunged once more; he missed. "Aveen! Wait!"

An immense black shadow came from nowhere. It swept over the distant trees, careened along the creek, and then hovered over them both.

Aveen drew up short, stared at the blackness where it covered her feet, then turned frightened eyes to Del.

A growl rumbled through the air around them.

Del looked up to find muddy brown dragon wings battering the air, and curving dragon claws plummeted toward him.

"Run!" He burst into speed and tried to capture Aveen at the same time.

An orange fireball erupted in front of him, cutting him off.

His hand found Aveen's arm, though, and he pulled with all his strength, turning to sprint away from the fire and take Aveen with him.

She stumbled around beside him, but he kept moving.

Another flame geyser hit the ground near their

feet.

Del swerved and ran straight for the pool at the bottom of the waterfall.

Aveen lost her footing and tumbled, but Del kept his grip on her.

He dragged her along the ground, his gaze fixed on the water. "Take a deep breath!" His toes reached the edge of the water just as Aveen gasped. He sucked air deep into his lungs. Then he plunged headfirst, Aveen in tow.

He flailed his arms and legs, trying to plummet them both deeper.

Aveen struggled too, her little feet kicking. They weren't going to get very far before they'd both have to surface for another breath.

He spun in the water to find her face, to try to communicate, but she was wrenched right out of his hands.

She screamed. The sound bubbled and distorted around him.

He grabbed at her, and his head broke the surface of the water.

This time when she screamed, it was clear and high. "Del!"

"Aveen!"

She was above him, dangling upside down from a brown dragon claw.

"Del!"

He rushed onto the shore and leaped up, and their fingers brushed. "Aveen!" He jumped again, but she was too far. He tried again and again, but she was swept away toward the sky. "No! Don't take her!"

Something hit him hard on the head and dropped with a splash into the water. He was too numb to acknowledge it, he could only stare at Aveen's young face as it drew farther and farther away from him.

The dragon raised a screech that sounded painfully like a victory taunt. Then it veered off over the waterfall.

"No," Del moaned. "No."

He watched Aveen's eyes until the dragon crested the cliff. Then waterfall spray obscured her face, and the high trees on the mountainside embraced her with their branches.

She was gone.

He lingered in the water, staring off at the sky and feeling swallowed up by eerie emptiness.

Then a glimmer caught his eye. A metallic circle floated beside him, with a chain that drifted like a silver snake on the water.

The medallion Aveen had been carrying. He picked it up.

"Go," came a whisper, like a ripple over the pool. "Fault."

"I know it's my fault," Del moaned, too brokenhearted to realize he was talking to himself.

"Go," the whisper urged. "Climb."

Del turned his eyes to the waterfall, and to the shelving of rocks. But the water would knock him flat if he climbed! And if he did try, where would he go next, anyway? What did he think he was going to do?

As he stood there, dripping and puzzling, a quiet settled in. He looked around, trying to figure out what had changed. His eyes turned back to the waterfall. Or, what used to be the fall, for the water had stopped rushing, and the embedded rocks were already beginning to dry. He stared.

He draped the medallion around his neck. Then, without understanding exactly why, or where he was going, he reached up and began to climb.

His hands scuffed on the stone cliff. His shirt caught as he dragged himself upward, and the material split wide. His feet struggled to find holds, and his biceps trembled from the strain.

When he reached the top, he was bloodied, torn, and exhausted. But he did reach the top. He flopped over onto prickly growth and closed his eyes.

"Go," came the whispers.

He grunted.

"North."

At first, he resisted, wanting to rest. Then he thought of Aveen. He sat up. He pushed to his feet. He strode forward.

He was walking on a plateau, as though the top of the cliff had been sheared off. Green elms swayed and rustled, interspersed with yellow and white vines clinging like netting to underbrush.

Behind him, the waterfall suddenly roared again, loud and strong, and drowned out what other wildlife noises might have kept him company.

He walked along the high creek's bank for a while,

until it made a sharp turn and disappeared into a hidden flow beneath the rock. There, at the edge of the plateau, he stared down at the drop-off. To keep going north, he would have to climb down and make his way to the next hill. It would take him days! How was he supposed to help Aveen?

He gripped the medallion, but it didn't seem to have any answers, either.

Tears threatened. He knuckled at his eyes.

When he opened them, something glinted at the edge of his sight. He blinked at the sky, trying to make it out. Wings. A swaying tail. A dragon! A green dragon was coming in fast and dipping to overtake him. He bolted for the cover of trees.

"Son of James," called a voice like the tumble of rocks down a hillside.

Del's ears twitched, but he kept running. He felt the dragon above him, and the stir of wind from massive wing tips.

"Your people have reached the moors to the west."

Del stumbled to a halt. He dared to look up, shading his eyes with his hand. "How do you know?"

"I watched them. Reinforcements guard them." The dragon swooped and thrust out his wings to coast to a soft landing, just feet ahead.

Sunlight glimmered off the creature's fern-colored scales, dazzling them. Leathery wings tucked in, and the dragon turned a head as big as a hay bale. Yellow eyes the size of a saucer stared without blinking. Speckled fins rose from the center of his skull, arching outward at the tips. Del had never been so close to a dragon before. He could have touched its snout if he wanted. He didn't want to.

"Where is your sister?" the dragon asked.

"Aveen? She's my cousin." Del clutched at the medallion around his neck. "A dragon came. I tried to fight."

"She's been taken?" The dragon's wings burst from its back. "Hurry. Come."

Del hurried. He approached the dragon's side to find a saddle on its back. Four sets of handholds and footholds were sewn into the leather. He grabbed a pair and clung.

With a lurch, they went airborne. Del felt the ground drop away, and he gripped, trying to find his breath.

Eventually, he settled into the rhythm, and just closed his eyes.

"Where are we going?" He tried to shout toward the dragon's head, but he could barely hear himself in all the wind.

"Abbot's Fault," boomed the dragon.

"Where?"

"Abbot's Fault. The Tirchess dragon will have taken her there."

"Why?"

"Because that is where the chancellor will be."

"Chancellor? What chancellor?" Del opened his eyes but didn't look down.

"The one who brought the war to your village." The

dragon banked, and then careened across gentle slopes of wide moors, toward a ruined cluster of gray stone buried into a clough.

He landed gently inside the valley of the clough, but Del lost his grip anyway. The leather handles slipped from his clammy hands, and he tumbled hard onto the flat ground. He was going to be covered in bruises tomorrow.

When he stood up to brush dirt from his backside, he saw the castle tower they'd landed next to. It appeared to be what was left of a grand entrance hall, but little else remained besides stacks and mounds of fallen brick. Either the rest of the castle had been carved beneath the moors, or the moors had claimed it long ago. The moors claimed everything, eventually. That's what his mother often said.

"Where are we?" Del asked, creeping forward.

"Abbot's Fault. This is where the artifact will be stolen."

"You think Aveen is in there?" Even as Del asked the question, he felt the medallion quiver.

The dragon didn't respond. He was watching the sky.

"Go," said the whispers.

Del took a step. "Let's get her!"

The dragon held up a claw. "Don't rush. Your mage has gone to great lengths to hide. There are others going to greater lengths to retrieve him." He looked toward the gaping entrance of the ruined castle, his snout quirked.

"My mage?" Del didn't know any of those. Not in Cooperborough. Beasts and magic were commonplace in the larger towns and cities, but the only kind of professions in the outer territories were farming and mining, and nobody needed magic for that.

"I can't smell how many are inside," the dragon said.

"What do you mean, *my* mage?" asked Del.

The dragon shifted his gaze to Del's face.

"I think I'd know if there was a mage in my own village," Del said.

"Dress a mage in a cotton shirt and straw hat, and he is just another farmer," said the dragon with a tilt of his head. "And farming is a dangerous vocation. It can explain away many things."

"What do you mean?"

"Injuries are common, yes? Scars and such?"

Del snorted. "Well, sure. You should see the lump on my leg where I got stuck with a pitchfork last summer. My father is a legend with all his marks, head to toe. He and Uncle Randy argue a lot about who's toughest." Then Del remembered. "Used to argue, anyway."

"Uncle Randy?"

Del nodded. "Randall. My mother's brother."

"With a scar on his right palm that usually wins the arguments?"

Del narrowed his eyes on the dragon. "He says he grabbed a branding iron to keep it from falling on Aveen when she was crawling in the barn."

"A branding iron in the shape of a dragon's tail winding around a hill?"

"It's a snake around a..."

Scaly ridges above the dragon's eyes arched, and Del thought he looked amused.

"How'd you know about that, anyway?" asked Del.

"Six years ago, an artifact was taken during a goodwill mission between Tirchess and Gellwydra dragons." The dragon pushed off to advance toward the castle. "The first of many betrayals by your mage."

Del hurried to keep up. "My uncle hates magic! It's why he came to Cooperborough to begin with. Why would he take something that belongs to dragons?"

The dragon paused, glanced once more toward the sky, and then continued lumbering forward. "That's a good question. You should ask him yourself."

§

Del crept into the dark gateway behind the green dragon. At a turn in a hall, the dragon paused.

Del stopped too. After a moment of strained listening, Del thought he heard a droning voice in the distance. If he squinted, he could just make out the flicker of orange torchlight.

Then he heard another voice. "Let me go!"

"That's Aveen!" Del darted forward.

The dragon pressed his paw to Del's chest. "Allow me," he said.

Del did as he was told. He limped on tired feet,

creeping along beside the dragon's sliding tail, until he came to the edge of a huge hall. Dangling torch chandeliers glittered with flamelight that made the place seem brighter than it should be.

In the cavern, two dragons, a muddy-looking brown one and another like the color of dried hay, crouched with their backs to him. Between them stood a man in robes, waving his arms over a stone-carved pedestal. Atop the pedestal sat a large basin of water. Sitting in the basin, encased with leather rope, was Aveen.

"Let her go!" Del darted past the green dragon.

The brown dragon spun, slapping a paw in front of Del's foot. The creature curled back its upper lip to release a warning puff of smoke.

"Brackish," came the rumbling voice of the green dragon from behind Del. His muzzle lowered protectively over Del's shoulder.

The brown dragon recoiled, her yellow eyes snapping angrily. "The child will not be harmed if you do not interrupt."

"She doesn't know anything about a mage or an artifact," said Del.

The brown dragon's eyes narrowed on him. "But you do."

"He knows what I have told him," said the green dragon, right next to Del's ear. "The human children are innocent, as is the village you attacked."

"We were after the mage," said the brownish one.

The green dragon exhaled a gravelly rumble. "You

have brought your war to a land that is not a part of it."

The brown one sneered. "They are part of it now."

"Enough!" The robed man suddenly shouted. He lowered his arms. He turned to face them all. "Your bickering is distracting. And this child is useless."

"I told you," said Del. He stepped forward to pull Aveen out of the basin, but the brown dragon thrust out a paw to stop him. Del tripped over the dragon's toes. The medallion bounced out from beneath his shirt and caught torchlight.

The man narrowed his eyes, and then lunged for Del, grabbing at the disk. "You little whelp."

Del felt the chain break against his neck. He staggered away from the giant paw, but the brown dragon was still glaring down at him. He swiped at the medallion, trying to get it back.

The green dragon held back Del with a single digit. "Let it go," he said quietly to Del.

"Put it on the child," the robed man said.

The straw-colored dragon, still silent, lifted the medallion in a claw and draped it around Aveen's neck. Aveen watched Del, her eyes frightened and confused.

"It's going to be all right, Aveen," said Del, even though he had no idea what he was talking about.

The man raised his hands, and began to chant, this time with more vigor. Shortly, he stopped. He smiled. "Found him. You may remove the child."

The tan-colored dragon took the medallion off Aveen again, then hoisted her from the basin and set her on the floor. Del ran forward to hug her. Then he yanked at her bindings. "It's all right. Don't be scared," he said, because she was trembling while Del's hands worked at the leather rope around her wrists. Or maybe it was Del who was trembling.

Near them, on the pedestal, the basin water drew up into an arch.

Del froze, watching, as it shifted into a vague, transparent shape of a man. Watery arms reached down toward Aveen, and the shape released a pitiful wail of torment.

Del fell back, pulling Aveen with him.

Aveen pushed off and scrambled to her feet. "Daddy!"

Del blinked. He glanced at the green dragon, and then to the others.

Everyone stared as the water shape swirled and turned murky, as though someone had thrown a bucket of fireplace ash into it. Then the murk turned colors—flesh, green, brown—and collapsed into a man in wet clothing, sprawled across the now-empty basin. He twitched, breathing hard.

"Daddy," said Aveen. She reached up for his limp hand and pressed it to her cheek.

"Uncle Randy?" Del gaped.

"Where is the artifact?" The robed man snarled and hefted Uncle Randall out of the basin, knocking it from the pedestal. He dropped him hard to the floor as the basin clattered beside him.

Uncle Randall groaned. "I'm sorry, Aveen. I'm so sorry." He reached his scarred hand toward her.

A click sounded under the fallen basin. It was the gold medallion, opened into halves like a locket. Inside the halves lay another disk, this one dark and stone-like, imprinted with a design of a dragon tail winding itself around a mountain. An exact duplicate to the scar on Uncle Randall's palm.

The robed man dove for the disk. The green dragon spat flame and slapped his paw over the disk.

The man howled in pain, held his singed hand against his chest. "Brackish!" he cried. "Delphum!" He turned to hurry past Del and the others, but the green dragon clasped him around the neck and yanked him to the cold floor.

The brown dragon, and the straw-colored one who had come with the robed man weren't going to help him. They stared, looking caught, surprised, and trapped all at once. The green dragon turned a snarl toward them, and they both, in unison, fell back.

"Help me," said Uncle Randall, weakly. Del reached toward him, seeing him as a stranger.

The green dragon turned back to Uncle Randall when he spoke, and Del saw from the corner of his eye, and heard, the Tirchess dragons skulk backward into the darkness where torchlight couldn't reach.

"I'm sorry, Del," said Uncle Randall, still lying on the floor. "I only took a piece of it," Uncle Randall said. "A small part."

"But it wasn't yours to take," said the green dragon. "Nor is it yours, Chancellor Hallsworth." He lifted the robed man to make him stand on his tiptoes. "You've both brought violence to Gellwydra because of it."

Uncle Randall tried to stand, his clothes clinging and dripping puddles. Aveen pressed her face to his hands, quietly crying.

"My father was almost burned alive," said Del, his own anger seeping through to his words. "Because of some stupid thing you stole?"

Uncle Randall finally made it to his feet. "I only meant to borrow it. Believe me, Del, I wouldn't have wished harm to anyone. I was going to use it and return it, but I..." He lowered his gaze to Aveen, his eyes sad. "I couldn't bring myself to do it."

"Do what? What did you want it for?" Del asked.

"The artifact is a time key—" Chancellor Hallsworth tried to say, but the green dragon tightened his grip on the man's neck, cutting off his words. The man gasped for breath.

Just then, the cavern floor rumbled. Sounds of an avalanche, muffled through the castle walls, battered the ground so that Del had to grasp at Aveen to help her stay on her feet.

"Our reinforcements," said Uncle Randall.

§

Outside, twelve dragons were amassed, awaiting instructions. Wings beat restlessly, and claws scratched at earth and mud.

"Break into groups of three and search the east skies. Brackish and Delphum served the Chancellor, but there are many more," said the green dragon. He pushed the robed man forward. "Chancellor Hallsworth will no doubt be a great help in identifying them." Then the green dragon lifted his head. "Arkyl, you take the Chancellor to the High Congress and see it done. I'll take the human children to Shersborough, where their family awaits."

"I will go with you, Rennwyss," said a dragon pushing through the group, her lavender-speckled scales shuddering with each step like wind-ruffled heather. "To see the human travelers to safety beyond the mountains."

The bright green dragon nodded as the rest of the dragon host lunged skyward. The one called Arkyl pulled the robed man into the sky. Wings stabbed the air. Powerful, scaled bodies swerved into groupings. Claws flexed, and they parted, following their orders.

The green dragon turned his yellow-orange eyes to Uncle Randall.

Uncle Randall frowned. He passed a hand over his russet hair. Then he knelt before Aveen. "I won't be staying with you just now. Uncle James and Aunt Margaret will take care of you."

"I don't want to be without you!" Aveen gripped Uncle Randall's shirt.

"I know. But I have to..." His voice broke, and he closed his eyes.

"Why'd you take it, Uncle Randy?" Del looked from his uncle to the dragon. "What's a time key?"

"It unlocks a passage in time," said the dragon. "It's

most often used to return to a decision, or a choice, that one wishes to undo."

"I missed your mother so much, Aveen," said Uncle Randall. "I wasn't thinking straight. I wanted to go back. To save her."

Aveen sniffled. "It's all right, Daddy."

A tear traced through the dust on Uncle Randall's face.

"Let's give them some privacy," said the green dragon, and he lumbered to the clough ledge. "He may not be seeing Aveen for some time."

"What's going to happen to him?" Del asked.

"Stealing magic has a hefty penalty, but I believe his grief clouded his judgment. I will tell this to the senate members."

"We lost good dragons because of him," said the lavender-speckled dragon, following them. "The Senate will not go easy."

Del shifted his weight, watching Uncle Randall from this distance. "You know," he said, looking up to the dragons, "He never talks about how Aunt Lyla died. No one does."

"In childbirth," the bright green dragon said.

Del blinked at the dragon's somber face. "Childbirth? Because of Aveen?"

The dragon regarded Del for a time, and then turned his face to watch Uncle Randall look toward them.

"When I was standing at Aveen's house, while it was burning," Del said. "I thought I saw someone.

Someone who looked a lot like Uncle Randy, but it couldn't have been."

"No?" asked the green dragon.

"He was old," said Del.

The dragon didn't reply. He just watched Uncle Randall and Aveen as they quietly talked.

Uncle Randall was holding Aveen's hand, and his jaw was tight. But his eyes were clear, and he looked serene.

"For a man about to face a harsh punishment, he seems peaceful," said the lavender dragon.

"Peaceful," said the green one. "Yes."

"Even though he's had his choice taken away from him," the other dragon said.

The green one gave a thoughtful sort of rumble. "Perhaps *because* his choice has been taken away from him."

Uncle Randall walked over, then, and scooped Aveen back onto his hip. "We're ready."

Del clutched at the straps of the green dragon's saddle, feeling better prepared this time for lift off. Looking forward to it, even. He lifted himself into the front seat.

Aveen found her hold, and Uncle Randall did the same, sitting behind her to steady her.

"Keep looking forward," Del said.

Uncle Randall smiled.

A River

A river

cuts into the bank

changing the land

and

in time

its own path

THE TIME SCAR
PART TWO

Clamp heard the sound before Aveen; he went rigid. His hackles raised. He didn't growl, but Aveen threw herself behind Cow Rock, the massive, bovine-shaped boulder along the edge of Ilsey Moor. Maybe her bulldog could smell the difference between dragons, but Aveen couldn't, not even after all this time. They sounded, smelled, and looked all the same to her. Gigantic. Powerful.

Deadly.

This dragon landed almost soundlessly onto the open field of blooming heather, and Clamp's stubby tail wagged.

Evening fog was just crowding out the cool sun, but Aveen could see the dragon's lichen-colored legs, thick like logs, pushing through heather mounds several feet away. His pace was steady, determined. Moorland dragons were rumored to have even-tempered, calming sorts of dispositions, but magical beings, any kind of magical being, were too unpredictable to Aveen. She was busy trying to judge the dragon when he spoke.

"Hello, little companion," said the dragon to Clamp.

Clamp went excited. His jowls slobbered, and his entire backside wiggled as he weaved in and around the dragon's legs.

"Traitor," Aveen said to Clamp, crawling out from behind the rock.

"He knows I mean you no harm," said the dragon.

Aveen recognized him, then. Rennwyss.

It's true, he'd always been kind, and he'd saved her aunt and uncle long ago, during the bloody border war. She remembered, even though she'd been so young. It should have been enough to prove him trustworthy, but it wasn't. Somehow, for Aveen, it just wasn't. Even as the dragon lowered his chin and tilted a smile toward her dog.

"A good little bodyguard." He patted Clamp's head with an enormous green paw.

Aveen watched Clamp hunker, then roll to his back, waving his legs. Clamp's tongue lolled out, blissful.

"Mm-hmm," Aveen said, shaking her head at Clamp.

Twilight dusted the sky; it filtered in around them, bringing shadows and glowbeetles. One luminous creature flitted near the dragon's face, and the shine reflected in the deep yellow-orange of his eye and glimmered the scales across his brow. And it deepened the seriousness behind his expression.

"But you're not here to visit Clamp," said Aveen. "Are you?"

"No." The dragon's haunches settled. He met her gaze. "Your father is dying."

The words slapped her, made her dizzy. "My father?"

The dragon nodded.

She'd assumed her father was already long gone, buried in the potter's field for people who died in prison. She collected herself, tried to sound unbothered. "And?"

"And he wishes to see you."

She might have laughed, if not for the bitterness in her throat making it impossible. "Typical." She turned to trudge back home and whistled for Clamp.

Clamp came to her side, panting, and Aveen rubbed his ear.

"My father forced me over and over to deal with his long absences without warning, without goodbyes," Aveen said. "He resurfaced when he wanted to in the same way. Never so much as an explanation. I closed the door on him a long time ago." Aveen nudged Clamp to lead on, and she took a step to follow him home. "Please tell my father I said so."

"Tell him yourself," said the dragon.

She glanced over her shoulder to say something even more firm and convincing, but two things happened at once; a figure came out from behind the dragon's shoulder, and Clamp growled.

The faint light made the man's gray eyes bright and his white hair dull. He favored a hip. His feet shuffled. An old man. He was a virtual stranger to her, especially as dramatically changed as he was now, but she immediately recognized him. "Daddy," she said.

Clamp continued to growl in warning.

She let him.

"Aveen," said her father, his voice thin like water. "I've missed you."

"Yes," she said. "You've missed everything."

He was silent for a long moment. He outstretched an arm toward Clamp, who looked up at Aveen for a signal.

Aveen considered, then nodded.

Clamp crept forward and gave her father's left hand a sniff.

That's when Aveen noticed her father was wearing a glove on his right hand. The same kind of glove for as long as she could remember.

"Have you come to tell me you're sick?" asked Aveen.

"Yes, in a way," her father said.

"Is that why the dragons released you?"

Her father looked at Renwyss.

The dragon arched the ridges above his eyes and a look was exchanged between them she didn't understand.

Then her father turned to her again. "They had already released me."

"What?"

"I've been in Elonra, in the capital, working with Renwyss…" He nodded toward the dragon, "…and the Bureau."

The Bureau for Human Assistance in Dragon Affairs. Part of the Gellwydra dragon government. "For how long?" Aveen asked.

He hesitated. "Six years."

She took a step back. She looked from the dragon to her father. "And you never even…?" Then she caught herself. Even now, she was still surprised. Stupid. She spun away and began again to walk toward home. "Come on, Clamp."

"Aveen," her father called. "There's more you don't understand."

"Oh, I know," she said. "I'll never understand."

Her father was suddenly beside her. His wrinkled hand clutched her arm and pulled her to a stop. "Please. Give me a minute."

His physical touch flared hot anger in Aveen. She yanked free and whirled on him. "The day of my eleventh birthday, do you know what I did? I decided to grow up. Just like that. I went to bed a child, full of hope that the next day you'd be there. That somehow, unexplainable magic would happen, and you'd materialize, because maybe my birthday was special enough. Maybe being eleven was special enough. Maybe something, anything, about that day would make a difference."

"Aveen—"

"But, no. No father. No letters. No messages of

any kind. Nothing." She stabbed her finger toward the dragon. "From the moment *he* came into your life there was never anything special about me, and I finally accepted it. You had let me go, so I let you go, too. I turned eleven, and I grew up."

Clamp circled them both restlessly. His paws crinkled low, grassy leaves, making the only sound between them for several moments.

"I meant to be there," he finally said. "In your doorway."

She regarded him. His eyes were damp.

Hers were dry.

"Let me come with you now. We'll talk," he said.

A small voice inside her did cry out, trying to be heard. It wanted to say *yes, all is forgiven, let's be a family again*. But she'd listened to that voice before, followed it many times to the broken, lonely place that inevitably came.

"I wish you well," she said. Then she turned once more for the path, and walked beside Clamp without stopping, all the way from the damp of the heathered moor until her feet found the rocky edge of the city's pavement, and on into the orange light of her street's lamplights.

Inside, in her small apartment studio, in the cool, summer darkness, she locked the door behind her.

§

In the morning, Aveen wandered distractedly

through Shersborough. Her neighborhood felt oddly unfamiliar, despite activities continuing as typically as ever.

Shan Ramer and his two boys chased stray dogs out of their raised vegetable patch; she wondered again why they never repaired their fence.

Uncle James argued pleasantly with his neighbor, Greg Donnis, over the fair trade of lemon peas for juneberries; he waved when he spotted her. Her cousin, Del, sat on the front stoop of their fieldstone home, reading a book.

The ground rumbled from steam cars and horse hooves. The distant canal gorged the air with moisture, and the sun tried hard to bake it dry before midday. It was the same place as usual. And yet, it wasn't.

Lolly Donnis sprinted toward her from behind his home, one of the few single-family buildings in the borough. He was waving a poster. He kicked up puddles with his boots, and by the time he reached her, his jeans were muddy. He was always excited about something that way; too distracted to mind if his hair was combed or his shirt collar was folded. Even his nickname, Lollygag, was a sidetracked accident; his father was always accusing him of lollygagging, and the name just sort of stuck.

"Aveen," he called, skidding across wet cobbles. "My father's taking us downtown. Have you seen the poster?" He stuck the paper under her nose.

She leaned back, took it from his hand, and turned it around. It was a poster featuring garish faces, all with too-big smiles and colorful, glittery makeup. Beneath the image was an announcement. "Carnival?" she asked.

"Yes," Lolly said. "Performers. Want to come? My dad will buy your ticket if I ask him."

"Is your brother going?" Aveen asked.

Lolly's brother was younger, short-tempered, and too much like Lolly's father for Aveen's taste.

"We could leave him home," Lolly said.

"That wouldn't be very polite," said Aveen. "…but thank you." She wasn't in much of a smiling mood, but she smiled for Lolly. His warmth tended to rub off on her. On everyone.

"Something is bothering you," he said.

She almost denied it, but he wouldn't believe her, and would manage, the way he usually did, to wrangle the confession out of her anyway. "Let's walk," she said.

He stuffed the parchment into his jeans and took her hand.

She liked the feel of his wide palm, how it was toughening over time into the hand of a working man.

He led her around the Ramers' garden and toward the park, into an unpaved field of cotton grass.

"I saw my father last night," she said, when they were a distance into the field.

He stopped short. "Your father?"

She nodded.

"I thought he was in prison," said Lolly. "Or dead. Or dead in prison."

"So did I," said Aveen. "But he's been in the capital, apparently. Working with the Gellwydra government."

He stared at her, his brows upraised, his dark eyes focused. It was the longest time he'd been quiet and still since she'd known him. Then he bent over, plucked up a stalk of grass, and stuck it between his teeth. "Can I meet him?"

"Can you *meet* him?!" She yanked her hand from his grasp.

"I just… I'd like to go with you next time you see him," he said.

"There isn't going to be a next time," said Aveen.

"Oh." He chewed on the end of his stalk. "Why not?"

She stared at him. "Why *not?*"

He smiled. "You're like an echo today."

She gave him an exasperated push.

A chime rang out from across the field, then a voice. "Nilsin! Nilsin Donnis!"

"There's your mother," said Aveen. Lolly's mother was the only one who still called him by his birth name. And the only one in the whole town who still used an old bell cable to communicate.

"I'd better go. Think about coming with us tomorrow." Lolly spit out his blade of grass, and then ran off.

Aveen watched the wet grass land on white flowers on the ground, on a small patch of dark shadow. The shadow shifted shape, and Aveen recognized wings, and in that same moment, knew who it was. She looked up to find an oncoming dragon, his scales a splash of glittering absinthe against the sky.

He didn't land, but swooped to tip his wings and sail off toward the nearest grove of trees.

She almost didn't go. But she was halfway there already, and having two visits from the dragon in two days was unusual enough to feel urgent.

When she reached the trees, Rennwyss emerged without a greeting. "Quickly, you must come with me."

"Why?"

"The town is being watched," the dragon said. "We must lead them away."

In an instant, her memory erupted in flames, in shouts, in screaming panic. Soot-blackened faces flashed by. She smelled blood. She tasted fear. She'd been so young when the border wars dragged violence through her little village of Cooperstown all those years ago, but she remembered. Always in flashes. Always, without wanting to.

She moved quickly toward the dragon. He wore a saddle across his back, with long leather handles. Aveen gripped them and hoisted herself into the seat. It was her first time on a dragon saddle. "Who is watching the village?" she asked. "The same dragons as last time?"

"The same," said the dragon.

"I thought they wanted my father."

Rennwyss's wings thrust outward, and she felt their power in the blast of air against her face. "They did," he said, and crouched to launch. "Now they want you."

§

She buried her face against the dragon's spine, squeezing her eyes closed and swallowing back her nausea. She tried to imagine herself astride a horse, instead of a hundred feet in the air, careening through the sky at a speed never meant for human experience. Her hair whipped hard against her neck and head, her skirt snapped against the back of her legs, her hands cramped from gripping the leather handles. Just when she was on the verge of begging him to put her down… he did.

He landed with a gentle bump.

She sucked in a breath before she finally opened her eyes.

They were back in the moors, farther outside of town than she'd ever walked. She knew them, recognized them, although they looked completely different here, compared to what she could barely see of them even on a clear day in Shersborough.

From town, when patchy fog burned away and the sun was high and bright, she could see the green, velvety curves of the moors that often made her think of the humped spines of the very dragons that lived there. She wondered if, every now and again, one ridge simply woke up, broke away, and began flying, and joined his dragon family in the sky.

She took a closer look around them. The heather was sparse here, with patches of scrabble dirt that got wider toward the east, until they met up to form a dirt valley that became a clough. Down the ravine of the clough, the dirt led to a hunched, half-ruined old building, that from here looked like an abandoned pile of gray brick and rusted ironwork.

Abbot's Fault.

Disjointed, flashing memories came at her again. During the war, after the violence in the village, she'd been taken. Flown in dragon claws, bound with leather. Brought to a castle. This castle.

"Why are we here?" she asked, her voice a whisper.

"Your father awaits us." The dragon walked forward.

Aveen clung to the straps on his back, her grip turning white. "I don't want to go in there."

"I know," he said, leading her toward the black throat of the entrance hall, whose doors had long been battered open.

Inside, her eyes adjusted slowly. So did her memories. Before, there was torchlight. Not this time. Before, the hall was bright and dry. Now, the air tasted of stale water and dragged stickiness across her skin.

"Rennwyss?" asked her father's voice from the dark.

"Yes, Randall Elmwood. Step to your left."

Aveen felt the dragon's ribs swell with breath.

He blasted a stream of fire. A stone-filled pit illuminated, then caught flame. Above the pit, a torch chandelier ignited, which shot its light to another, and to another, in a glowing ring above the pit, and the cave became warm and bright as daylight.

Her father stood beside the blazing fire pit, his shoulders hunched, his gaze lowered. "I never meant for it to come to this, Aveen."

She unpeeled her grip from the dragon's saddle and lowered herself to the cave floor. "Is anyone going to tell me what is going on?"

Her father looked up at the dragon, then back to her face. "I've been staying away to keep you safe. But now, because I… well. A moment of weakness. Now I've led them to you."

It took a long moment for his words to sink in. "You've stayed away," she repeated.

"To keep you safe," he said again.

"Safe from what, exactly?" she said. She looked first at the dragon, and then at her father. She was worn right through from all the lying, the flying, and the bits of story too small to make any kind of sense. "Once and for all. What is going on?"

It was the dragon who stepped forward. "You remember what happened last time you were here?"

Of course she did. Blurry images, distant conversations. She remembered being placed into a large, golden bowl while she was still bound in leathers. Surrounded by leering dragons. Chanted over. Terrified. She felt her legs begin to tremble, her arms.

Rennwyss laid a reassuring paw against her back. "Those were Tirchess dragons, beneficiaries of Chancellor Hallsworth."

Aveen's father spoke up. "Hallsworth used you to force me into helping him."

"Your father stole a piece of an artifact from the Gellwydra dragons," said Rennwyss.

"A time key," said Aveen. She didn't realize she

remembered that part.

"Yes," said Rennwyss. "And Chancellor Hallsworth, from Tirchess, blackmailed him into using it for him."

"By cheating," said her father. "By starting a war." He balled his hands to fists and turned his back to them.

"And that's why you went to prison," Aveen said to him. She watched his shoulders rise and fall with breath. With shame. "But what does any of that have to do with me now?" she asked.

"All of time has everything to do with each moment," said Rennwyss.

Which didn't mean anything at all to Aveen.

Her father was still silent and brooding, so she kept her attention on the dragon.

"Think of traveling through time as though walking through a maze," Rennwyss said. "Endless possibilities to decide on and turn toward. With the artifact, Chancellor Hallsworth was able to enter passages to the past. He prevented births. Murdered outright. Eliminated moments in the future."

Her father finally spoke again. "Except it hasn't stopped. They lost their war, but all the meddling he… I…."

The dragon and her father exchanged another look.

"It's complicated," said Renwyss. "The effects of interference have been long lasting. The Gellwyrdian Senate felt it was a waste of energy, skills, and talent to allow your father to die away in our prison, when he could instead be helping us to track the Tirchessians' work. To correct it." The dragon came forward a step, nearer to her father. He swung his wide face over his shoulder to Aveen. "And your father protected what artifact pieces he could, under the circumstances."

"You mean, there are others?" asked Aveen.

The dragon smiled with a strange combination of humor and sadness. "Yes," he said. "And time magic is very seductive. And dangerous."

Her father released a long breath and wilted onto a fallen column near the rim of the fire pit.

She felt his weariness even from her distance. She sat, too, first brushing the dust away from a tilted stone. "How is it dangerous?" she asked.

"It is difficult to control the momentum caused by a single, minor change. To minimize it, you must enter a time passage—or door, if you will—as close as possible to the moment you wish to alter." The dragon leaned forward and scratched a claw against the floor, drawing in the dried mud. "Using each time key is its own puzzle with its own set of doors." He illustrated a box with connecting lines, interwoven as a maze. "With it, one cannot pass through walls. Once one enters a doorway, one can travel along that chain of events only."

"And you have to know how each moment affects the next to decide which one to interfere with," said her father. "If you take a wrong turn and branch off to a peripheral conclusion, you'll find a different moment than the one you're looking for. You have to backtrack and try again."

"I don't think I understand," said Aveen.

"Now now," said her father. "But you'll learn."

She looked up, and this time, found her father looking directly into her eyes. "Why?" she asked.

"Because you are going to take over where I leave off. You're going to be the next tracker."

"Me?" She felt heat climbing up her throat. She stared between her father and the dragon. "Take over?"

"Yes," said the dragon. "You must step into the maze."

§

Lolly fastened a lug nut onto the wheel stud of his dad's truck. It had been needing repair for a while, and with such a long trip to Elonra tomorrow, it couldn't be put off any longer. Feeling a job well done, he tossed the wrench near the jack on the ground and climbed into the truck bed to sit. He drew a small notebook from his pocket, then a nub of a pencil. He sketched.

He was just smoothing the edge of Aveen's cheek on the paper when frantic barking made him look up. It sounded like Clamp. The dog's call was high-pitched, excited. Maybe he'd cornered a squirrel.

Lolly slid from the truck bed and tucked his sketchbook away as he strolled across the street toward Aveen's apartment building. Her uncle James stepped onto the front stairs, wiping his hands on a cloth. Behind him, her cousin Del stepped outside, too. The door squeaked closed behind him.

"Something's got into that dog," said James.

"Yes, sir," said Lolly. "I was just going to see."

"Be careful," said Del. "Something feels off."

Suddenly a noise exploded, like someone tossed a fresh log onto a fire.

Clamp's barking turned to tortured howling before it went silent.

Lolly smelled charred meat. He snapped his gaze to James.

James' color drained.

Del looked up. He went pale, too.

A mud-colored, green-brown dragon rose over the shingle roof of the apartment building, and its shadow swallowed the whole front yard. It hovered there, wings beating, and let out a screech that raked Lolly's ears. The ground shuddered. Then the dragon suddenly stopped and sucked in a breath.

"Look out!" Lolly dove at James and knocked him off the stairs to the ground. He felt Del's weight crash down onto both of them.

Behind them, the steps burst into flame.

"Run, boys," hollered James, wrestling to disentangle.

Lolly heard Aveen's aunt Margaret calling from somewhere nearby. He rolled over to try to see her through smoke, but he felt claws scrape his cheek and clamp around his shoulder, and the ground drop away beneath him.

He was pulled into the sky. He dangled, helpless, as his feet scraped rooftops, then treetops.

Those mud-colored claws cut through his shirt, pressed hot pain into his skin.

He clenched his teeth, trying not to cry out. His stomach twisted. He went dizzy. Time seemed to move too fast for his brain to catch up.

The moors swerved into view beneath him, then went out of focus.

"Let me go," he tried to say, but with the rush of his heartbeat and the wind battering his ears, he wasn't sure the sound came out.

But he was released, suddenly. He hit the ground, jarring his legs. He collapsed into a heap, struggling for breath.

"Bring me the child," said the dragon. Who was it talking to?

Lolly looked up to see another, brighter green dragon emerging from a castle built into the side of a clough. First the snout, then the powerful head and neck. Before the bright green dragon was fully visible, it was rumbling a warning. "Do not do this, Brackish."

A man appeared from the same castle doorway to rest his hand on the green dragon's side. The dragon snorted flames.

"I will not give her to you," said the man.

"Father?" He heard Aveen's voice wavering from inside the fracture.

"Aveen?" Lolly pushed to his feet. A fist the size of a tree trunk batted his spine and knocked him flat again. Massive brown claws pressed his legs to the ground.

"What's happening?" Aveen darted out from the darkness, but the man gripped her arms and held her back.

The green dragon placed its foot in front of her.

"Lolly?" she called.

"Don't go, Aveen," said the man. "Whatever happens, you can't go to him."

"Then he'll die," said the mud-colored dragon, his voice rumbling like a thundercloud above Lolly's head.

"No!" Aveen kicked. She clawed. "Let me go!"

The man pushed her into the stone door frame and pressed his weight across her. "I won't," he said.

"Stay back," said Lolly, although he wasn't sure what was happening, either. He was afraid for himself, but afraid for Aveen, too.

Then the claws released him.

Surprised, he looked up at the brown dragon. Then he climbed to his feet.

"Run, Lolly!" cried Aveen. "Run!"

"No, Brackish," shouted Aveen's dragon. Green, powerful legs launched toward him.

Then, from behind, Lolly heard the explosion of a log being thrown onto a fire. Heat engulfed him, and again, he smelled charred meat.

§

Aveen screamed. She watched Lolly turn black inside a cocoon of flame, and she screamed.

The green dragon collided into the duller brownish one, cutting off the flame, and they thrashed upward into the air.

Her father yanked her arms, dragging her stomach

across granite stones.

Still, she screamed and screamed until her throat went hoarse and her lungs ached, and her body clenched with the effort.

Only when they were again inside the castle, near the pit, after her screams had turned silent from exhaustion, did her father release her. She went limp with grief.

"Aveen," said her father. "I'm so sorry."

"You killed him," she whispered, her face pressed against stone and dirt, her voice barely heard through her wrecked throat.

She heard his footsteps moving away, heard the scrape of something being pulled across the ground. "There is much I have to answer for," he said. "But I did not kill that boy."

"Lolly," she mumbled. "His name was Lolly."

"Brackish killed him, Aveen. Hallsworth used a time key to send that dragon on a path to you. When the dragon couldn't get to you, he killed that boy."

"Lolly," she said again, louder. She pushed up to sit and glared at her father where he sat on a square stone.

"The first time that dragon came through, he *did* kill you," he said.

She felt her glare dissolve. "What?"

"I led them to you. By accident. I thought I'd lost them. I had to risk it because I won't be able to do this much longer. I came to you last night to explain all this." He rested his elbows on his knees, and his shoulders sagged. "But they used me to find you. They tracked you and killed you in a field of white flowers, along with a boy in muddy jeans."

She shook her head, resisted what he was saying. His words passed through her, shivered her spine, made her feel suddenly transparent. She hugged her arms to herself to reassure she was still there. "But why?"

"Because you're important." He stood. His eyes deepened, developed an intensity she remembered. "You change things somehow, in the future. I've tracked them, tried to control Hallsworth and his dragons. But you... you *conquer* them."

"Me?"

"You become better at this than I ever could."

It unnerved her, the way he spoke of things in past tense that hadn't even happened yet.

"So is it true? What you said to me last night?" he asked.

"Is what true?"

"That you've grown up. Or are you still really a child, and still angry at me for failing you?"

She regarded him a long time, his face rugged with age, his eyes weak and unfamiliar. "I'm not a child," she finally said.

The green dragon stumbled in then, from around a corner in the halls. Light splayed over his wounds; scales torn from his chest, blood coursing from his mouth. He favored his right front foot. "It is safe again," he said.

Aveen looked from the dragon to her father. "In the maze, I can undo the things the chancellor has done?"

Her father nodded.

"And you'll teach me?" she asked.

"If you'll trust me," he said.

She walked to her father, her thoughts on Lolly, her decision made. "Show me," she said.

§

It was a long night of too much talking. Aveen wanted into the magic, eager to find Lolly, but her father insisted she repeat phrases over and over, over and over, until she thought she'd go mad with the monotony.

"I have to choose the correct passage and follow it to the correct conclusion," she droned. Her hands were pressed to her face. She was sprawled on her back on the floor of the castle. "If I discover I've entered the wrong path, I return to the beginning and try again."

"But if it's the correct passage, what do you do?" asked her father.

She pushed up to sit. "How many times do I have to say this?"

"At least once more," he said.

She groaned. "Fine. If I'm in the correct passage, I'm allowed to prevent only those circumstances that were changed by the other time dragons."

"You must understand this above all else, Aveen Elmwood," said the green dragon, who crouched near her. He lowered his snout to find her gaze, and when their eyes met, she felt the weight of it as though a hand reached through her skin to press against her soul. She shifted, uncomfortable.

"Once you experience the maze, you will realize your power," the dragon continued. "Your action, or failure to act; a simple word spoken where previously none had been; even an expression on your face; all these things can divert choices and change events, subtle as a dove's breath now, but drastic beyond comprehension at the end of the passageway."

As he spoke, his eyes darkened. She saw her reflection in them, sensed the memory of her death in them. She shivered.

"You must learn the future as it should be, so you can know how to revert the past to its proper path," said her father. "For now, you will only observe." He stood, gripped her hand, and pulled her to her feet. "Observe. Do you understand?"

She nodded.

"First, we will return," he said.

"To where?"

"To the doorway," said her father. "We're in a time passageway now. I opened it to find your death and to prevent it. We can't open another until we've returned to where we entered."

Aveen touched her head to her brow, rubbing at a growing headache. "I don't know if I'll ever fully comprehend," she mumbled.

"You will," said the dragon, and rested his paw against her back. "You will master it." He smiled.

He spoke with such conviction, she almost believed him.

"One day, you will come to trust me," he said.

She almost believed that, too.

"Right, off we go," said her father.

She moved to follow, but the dragon patted her back before he withdrew his paw. "Not you," he said. "Wait here."

"Wait here?"

"Your father and I must return, not you," the dragon explained. "You will see in a moment."

Just then, in the near distance, her father removed his glove to reveal a mossy stone held against his palm. It glowed faintly, and he pointed it toward the wall. The dragon moved first, lumbering toward the wall but slowly disappearing, head to tail, before he reached it. Then her father stepped in behind, and they were both gone.

The next moment, their figures emerged from nowhere. A dragon head shape pressed through what looked like resisting membrane; it suddenly broke, spraying bog-like silt and water into the space. The water splashed onto ruined stonework, sizzled into the hot fire pit, and created a massive puddle on the floor. Then the bog water puddle pulled into itself, un-swirled its muddy colors into separate green and brown, and jettisoned upward into the distinct forms; dragon and man. Both shapes shuddered. One became Rennwyss, and the other her father. Both breathed heavily. Both dripped water as through they'd emerged out of the moors. The pebble in her father's palm wasn't glowing anymore.

"There we go," he said. "Back to square one." He

leaned forward to catch his breath.

"Except this time, I'm alive," she said.

Her father looked up. He nodded. "As it should be. So now it's your turn."

"Lessons are over?" she asked.

"Oh, no," he said. "Just beginning."

He offered the pebble to her. She held it between her thumb and forefinger. Then he held up his hand, showing her the scar on his palm: raised flesh, in the design of a dragon tail winding itself around a hill.

"You always told us it was from a branding iron," she said.

"It happened when I picked up the piece of artifact. In a way, it *was* a branding iron." He turned his palm, looked at it. "What I didn't realize until later is the artifact embedded magic into me at the time."

"That is what enables us to combat Hallsworth and his accomplices," said the dragon. "Elsewise, we would be at their mercy."

"But all this travel, all this magic rumbling through my blood… it's weakening. I'm getting old, and tired." Her father took her right hand and pressed his scar to her palm. "It's your turn. I think you're ready."

Aveen drew in a deep breath, thought again of Lolly. "I'm ready."

The dragon muttered a sound she didn't recognize. Suddenly, her palm burst with heat. She flinched, anticipating pain, but that didn't happen, just tingling, first in her hand, and then into her arm and upper chest. Her heart raced as though she'd run a mile. Her joints ached. Then, the tingling receded, and when it was all over, she bore a scar that encircled her upper arm; raised flesh in the design of a dragon tail wrapping itself around a hill.

"Do you hurt?" asked her father.

She shook her head. She saw her father's scar was gone. She ran her finger over the smoothness of his palm. "Do you?"

"No," he said. He smiled. "How would you like to open your first passage?"

She hesitated then, realizing she was afraid. Realizing how much was depending on her.

Lolly was depending on her. She braced her shoulders. "What do I do?"

"You need to know what moment in time you're revisiting, and to enter its passage at the closest point before it happened," said her father.

"Lolly invited me to a carnival this morning. I want to go back there."

"Where?"

"To his home."

Her father nodded and reached for the leather handles on the dragon's back. "Off we go, then."

§

They landed in a grove of trees not far from her own apartment. None of them had spoken on the trip; none of them were speaking now. It was a nervous silence. Aveen sensed that. As she released from the dragon's saddle, she decided against being the one to break it.

Her father did. "Observe only. You'll need practice before you can go off changing the world." He led her through thick branches to an area where the trees opened a little, and underbrush had been trampled flat. "You have the stone?"

She held up the pebble.

" It'll channel your magic to make a portal; a sort of chamber from which you'll choose your path. Since I'm now without the power, I can't go with you, but I'll send Rennwyss."

"But—"

"You're just practicing how to find the right passage. Now, lift the moss stone and focus on the moment you wish to change."

She did. Instantly she felt the tingle again. It crawled inside her skin, chewing on her muscles, gathering like ants toward her hands. She gasped, wanting to brush them off, knowing she couldn't.

There was a shift in the scene directly in front of her. A section of air shivered, went vaguely blurry. "I see it!"

Her father pressed her forward. "It will stay until you come back through. Don't be afraid."

She reached out to feel the air. It resisted. She glanced toward her father, and then to Rennwyss. The dragon nodded. "I am right behind you."

So she pushed; first her hand, and then her shoulders. The air broke against her, splashed wet against her face. She went dizzy and landed hard onto the ground.

"It is the coming and going that is hardest," said Rennwyss's voice behind her. "Once inside, you will dry. The doorways are effortless."

That's when she realized her dress dripped water as though she'd just dragged herself from the bog. She also realized how quiet it was. Oddly still, despite standing outside near her home, just as she was before.

But her father, who stood just inches away, was frozen. As were sparrows; some of them with wings extended above them, mid-flight. The wind was gone. The sun was high, but she couldn't feel it on her face.

"Oh," she said.

"Yes," said Rennwyss.

She looked up at the dragon. Water dribbled between his eyes; he shook it away. "What do I do now?" she asked.

"Choose."

She came to recognize blurry air patches surrounding them. Several. When she turned her head one way, more materialized. When she turned the other way, still more appeared.

She gripped the stone, hoping it would signal something, but when she held out her other hand, it wasn't the stone speaking to her, but her own heart. Not in words, exactly. More in the sense of humming along to familiar tune. She knew what sort of moment waited on the opposite side of the doorways, as if she'd been there before. "Not this one," she said. She moved on.

She passed her choices, circling in the quiet space, pausing here and there. Then she stopped altogether, and her gaze went to Rennwyss. "My father," she said. "He's on the other side of this one. He's looking for me."

"Be careful," said the dragon.

But she wanted to see. The patch of air came into sharp focus, opening itself. She stepped through it, feeling the sun again, hearing the birds. "He's looking for me," she said again.

She hurried through the trees, knowing where she was going, to her apartment, where she lived with Uncle James and Aunt Margaret. And she felt younger, as though the trees were taller and the earth newer. She missed her father.

She remembered it now. She was excited to see him. It was her birthday. She was turning eleven. She knew, somehow, her father was going to be there.

She heard voices. She veered to follow the sound. Just as she emerged from the trees, she felt a claw catch her dress's collar.

"Observe," reminded the dragon.

"You shouldn't have come," said Uncle James.

In that moment, she realized her uncle was talking to her father—the younger, bearded version of her father she remembered. The men stood at the back steps of the apartment building. Her father had one foot planted on a step and held a small, carved chest in his hands. Tears sprang into her eyes.

"I was careful not to be followed," said her father. "I want to explain to her. She's old enough to understand,

I think."

"Now?" Uncle James shook his head and reached for the box. "Think about it, Randy. Your sister and I have done all we can to protect her, raise her steady and safe. Telling her now will just stir it all up again, and you'll walk back out and leave her confused as ever."

Her father relinquished the box. His hands fell. "I just want to see her."

"Is that the right thing for Aveen? Are you sure she wants to see you?" Uncle James turned and climbed the stairs, one wrinkled hand gripping the chest, his other on the railing. "You think she wants you taking risks with her life every time you come around?"

"Yes," Aveen whispered from behind a tree. "Don't let him stop you, Father. Go find me."

Her father didn't speak again. Uncle James walked into the building, and the crooked door slapped shut. Her father lingered a little, then walked around the steps to a window. He peeked in. Then he walked between the building and the one next door, and disappeared.

Aveen darted out from behind the tree. "Wait!"

Rennwyss yanked her hard, and she tumbled backward, bumping into his leg and then flopping to the ground. "Forgive me," he said quickly. "But you cannot do the thing you wish to do."

"Let me go." She pushed to her feet. "He came to see me. I just want to make myself go to the window and look. I won't talk to him. I won't change anything."

"Yes, you will. That is exactly what you want to do. Change things."

She tried to disentangle the sleeve of her dress from his claw, but he gripped her arm and nearly lifted her off her feet. "If you do this," he said, his voice a soft rumble, "You will return to a world you do not recognize."

"I don't care. Put me down!"

The dragon drew in a long breath. Then he set her down and retracted his claw, freeing her.

The minute her feet touched ground she ran toward the building. But then, a boy came trundling toward her, swerving across the front yard and toward the back steps.

Aveen halted. She was exposed, conspicuous. She saw him fluff the orange petals of a fox rose in his hand, oblivious. His hair was damp, combed neatly back. The collar of shirt was neatly folded… but his trousers were splattered with mud.

Lolly. On his way with her birthday present.

She had forgotten about that part of the day. Aveen watched him now. Smiled. And then her own words echoed back through her mind.

I'm not a little girl.

She turned then and looked up again at Rennwyss's snout peeking out of the treeline. "You're right," she said. "This isn't the moment I came for. "Let's go."

§

Lolly Donnis finished helping his mother put away the breakfast dishes with a poster bitten between his teeth. Each time he carried a plate to the cupboard, he swerved past the window to search outside.

"Nilsin," said his mother, shaking her head. "You're going to wear a hole in my rug, worrying yourself at the window. Never you mind about the last of the dishes. Go find Aveen."

He spit the poster into his hand. "There she is now!" He galloped for the back door.

"But come back when you finished speaking with her," called his mother. "Your dad's needing help with the truck!"

"Yessum," he said as he slammed the door and bumbled down the steps. He was just about to turn the corner toward the front door when he heard a hiss.

"Pssst!"

He jerked to stop.

"Lolly, it's me, Aveen. Over here."

He spotted her crouching behind the truck that was lifted up on a jack, just outside their horse barn. He smiled, shuffling toward her. "Are we playing a game?"

"Yes, it's called 'get me into the horse barn without anyone seeing'."

"Never heard of that one," he said. But then, Aveen was one of the strangest girls he'd ever known, and it's what he liked about her. She *thought* things, had ideas. And she never minded him talking about his, either. "No one's coming now, if you want to run for it."

She peered over the top of the truck. "Are you sure?"

"I could throw a feed sack over your head and carry you in, if you want," he said.

She scowled. Then she dashed so fast even he almost didn't see it. He followed her, his boots noisy against the path.

Inside the horse barn, she nudged him. "Close the door."

He blinked, but obeyed.

She pressed herself against a stall. His horse, Donkey, reached his lips over the wall and nibbled at her sleeve. "No treat for you this time, Donkey," she said. "I'm sorry."

Lolly watched her pet his horse, watched her stroke Donkey's velvet nose with graceful fingers. Then she turned a smile over her shoulder at Lolly, and it took his breath. The way her smile always did.

That's when he noticed her arm, and the strange mark, like a vine, or a burn scar, that traced her upper arm and disappeared beneath her dress sleeve. How had he never noticed that before?

Their eyes met, and he knew she saw him notice. She didn't move to cover it or hide it. She just stepped toward him. Her smile changed, went soft in a way he'd never seen. She touched his cheek. "It's good to see you, Lolly. Really good."

"It is?"

She nodded. Her hand lowered. "I know about the carnival. I know you're going to invite me."

"How did you…?"

"Do you still want me to go?" she asked.

"Well, yes. But I—"

"I'll go if you promise me something."

He tucked the poster into the pocket of his jeans, searching her expression. "Something's bothering you."

She looked toward their feet. She leaned back against the stall, tucked her hands behind her hips.

"You're afraid," he said.

"Yes."

"Of me?"

She looked up, then. "Not the way you think."

"But it is me." He stepped back, his heart tightening.

Something was definitely different about her. She was tense, and deeply frightened; he saw it behind her eyes.

"Do you want me to leave?"

"No!" She grabbed his arms. "You have to stay. Promise you'll stay, no matter what happens or what you hear."

Clamp erupted in distant barking, startling him.

Panic flashed across Aveen's face.

"Can't you tell me what's happening?" Lolly asked.

"I don't know," she said. She waded through hay to peer out a window. She gasped.

He came to stand at her elbow. He gasped, too.

Over a grove of trees just behind the near apartment buildings, two dragons, one bright green and one dull, collided and thrashed in the air. Flames scorched treetops. Growls rumbled the ground.

People peered out windows or came to doorways to watch.

Lolly's father wandered a few steps down the road,

his shoulders stiff with alarm. He called to Clamp, who bounded toward him. Lolly's father bent, grabbed Clamp's collar, and led him off to safety inside their home.

Lolly moved toward the barn door.

"No!" cried Aveen, and she pressed him against the wall. "Don't go out there."

He spun to face her. "All right," he said. "You know what's happening, don't you?"

"Yes," she said. Tears glittered in her eyes.

He'd never seen her cry before, not in all the years he'd known her. It made him want to wrap his arms around her and smooth her hair. Tell her everything was going to be fine.

Sound cracked like a breaking tree, and the whole street shook with an impact.

Through the window, they watched the bright green dragon circle the trees, wings off-kilter.

Then he swooped directly for the horse barn. As he drew near, the noon sun lit his wounds; scales torn from his chest, blood coursing from his mouth. "It is safe again," he called, passing over the barn, his voice shuddering the structure.

Aveen leaned her forehead against Lolly's collarbone. "We did it," she said.

He didn't ask what. Not yet. He knew one of these days, she would tell him. But then he did wrap his arms around her.

She lifted her head. "I need to go." She didn't pull away.

He hesitated, wondering for the hundredth time how she would react if he tried to kiss her.

Then, *she* kissed *him*. Lightly. Quickly. On his mouth. And whatever he was about to say left his head and was replaced with a kind of empty-headed dizzy.

She smiled and slid the barn door open. His father was opening the door of the apartment building, Clamp at his heels. When the bulldog saw Aveen he charged toward her and rollicked around her feet.

"Come on, Clamp, you're going to get me seen. Let's go," she said.

"Hey," called Lolly, finally remembering what it was he was going to say. "You really going to the carnival with me?"

"Try stopping me," she said. She gave a smile and a little wave, then she turned the corner behind the barn.

§

Aveen hurried toward Rennwyss, where he was awaiting her in the trees just outside town. Clamp jogged along beside her, huffing and happily drooling.

"You did more than observe," said the dragon, as Aveen approached. She was expecting chastisement in his voice, but there was none.

"So did you," she said.

"I am becoming quite practiced at defeating Brackish."

"Thank you," said Aveen. "Lolly is very important to me."

"He is very important to the future of the Gellwyrda," said the dragon. "You will both need protecting in the times to come."

"Then it's a good thing we seem to work well together. Understand each other," said Aveen.

"Trust each other," said Rennwyss.

She nodded. She really was beginning to believe that possibility. "So. Off we go," she said, echoing her father. "To square one."

"Right," said the dragon.

Clamp sat on her foot. She bent down to scritch him on the chest. "Aw, don't worry, boy. I'm safe."

"She will return shortly, brave bodyguard," said Rennwyss.

Aveen gave Clamp one more hefty pat. "You'll see," she said. "It'll seem as though we never even left."

MORE FROM BIG IMAGINE

Explore our Films

Big Imagine doesn't only publish books. We make movies, too! Our film projects are circulating in festivals and are offered on streaming sites. We'd love to have you as a supporter!

bigimagine.com/films

MORE FROM BIG IMAGINE

Fantasy

Redheart

*Book One of the
Leland Dragons Series*

"Marvelous! Jackie Gamber has created a wondrous, enthralling world of adventure, mystery, and richly crafted characters. Dragons soar--and so do we! This is high fantasy at its most extraordinary."

- T. A. Barron,
New York Times bestselling creator of
The Merlin Saga and *The Great Tree of Avalon*

Redheart is available wherever books can be bought! Check your favorite retailers in both digital and print!

www.ingramcontent.com/pod-product-compliance
Lightning Source LLC
Chambersburg PA
CBHW061209210726
48294CB00006B/1800